TIME OF

UNDERSTANDING

Stories of Girls Learning
to Get Along with
Their Parents

SELECTED BY

HELEN FERRIS

FRANKLIN WATTS, INC.
575 Lexington Avenue, New York 22

ACKNOWLEDGMENTS

Thanks are due to the following authors, publishers, publications, and agents for permission to use the material indicated.

"Suddenly You're in Love," by Hila Colman, from *Ingenue*. Reprinted by permission of *Ingenue*. Copyright © by the author, 1960.

"Easter Present," by Rita C. Foster, from *Senior Prom*. Reprinted by courtesy of Parents' Magazine Enterprises, Inc. Copyright © 1951, by Parents' Magazine Enterprises, Inc.

"New Girl in Town," by Robert Paterson, from *The Ladies' Home Journal*. Reprinted by permission of Willis Kingsley Wing. Copyright © 1961, The Curtis Publishing Company.

"Medal for Mums," by Gertrude Crampton, from *Calling All Girls*. Reprinted by courtesy of Parents' Magazine Enterprises, Inc. Copyright © 1946 by Parents' Magazine Enterprises, Inc.

"Stop Calling Me Baby," by Lois Duncan, from *Seventeen*. Reprinted by permission of McIntosh and Otis, Inc. Copyright © 1962 by Triangle Publications Inc.

"The Reluctant Lilac," by Clae Waltham, from *Seventeen*. Reprinted by permission of the author. Copyright © 1962 by Triangle Publications Inc.

"The Autumn Heart," by J. P. Folinsbee, from *Senior Prom*. Reprinted by courtesy of Parents' Magazine Enterprises, Inc. Copyright © 1951 by Parents' Magazine Enterprises, Inc.

ACKNOWLEDGMENTS U. S.1215127

"Apron Strings," by Adele De Leeuw, from *Calling All Girls*. Reprinted by courtesy of Parents' Magazine Enterprises, Inc. Copyright © 1946 by Parents' Magazine Enterprises, Inc.

"Forbidden Yearning," by Margaret Craven, from *The Saturday Evening Post*. Reprinted by special permission of *The Saturday Evening Post*. Copyright © 1958 by The Curtis Publishing Company.

"Gather Ye Rosebuds," by Marion Dow, from *Seventeen*. Reprinted by permission of the author. Copyright © 1960 by Triangle Publications Inc.

"A Family Affair," by Jean Kinkead, from *Senior Prom*. Reprinted by courtesy of Parents' Magazine Enterprises, Inc. Copyright © 1950 by Parents' Magazine Enterprises, Inc.

"Written in the Stars," by Lois Duncan, from *Seventeen*. Reprinted by permission of McIntosh and Otis, Inc. Copyright © 1959 by Triangle Publications Inc.

"This Moment Forever," by Robert Zachs, from *Senior Prom*. Reprinted by courtesy of Parents' Magazine Enterprises, Inc. Copyright © 1950 by Parents' Magazine Enterprises, Inc.

"Behold," by Jean Fritz, from *Seventeen*. Copyright © 1958 by Triangle Publications Inc. Reprinted by permission of Russell and Volkening, Inc.

"Another Spring," by Michael Shaara, from *Redbook Magazine*. Reprinted by courtesy of the author and *Redbook Magazine*. Copyright © 1960 by Robert Shaara.

"Too Young to Marry," by John D. MacDonald, from *THIS WEEK Magazine*. Reprinted by permission of Littauer and Wilkinson. Copyright 1955 by the United Newspapers Magazine Corporation.

Lovingly and gratefully dedicated to
NORA BEUST *and* SALLIE MARKS
who understand

Understanding
Is a Two-Way Thing

WHEN one of your friends says, "My parents treat me as though I were a child, they can't seem to realize that I am growing up," you know just how they feel. And you sympathize with them when they add, "My mother and father are too strict. The rules they make for me are actually humiliating—about the time when I must get home at night from a date, for instance." And more than anything else, you wish that your parents could understand how you feel.

The girls in the stories in this book met this same situation. Tina's mother and father objected to the boy who invited her to go out with him in a racing car. Tina was most rebellious about that, but when she persisted in having her dates and an accident occurred, she was surprised by her parents' understanding. Karen cared deeply for a boy who was not at all interested in her. She thought the end of her world had come, until a talk with her mother made her realize that lots of girls go through the same experience, yet live happily ever after—with someone else.

Lynn's and Mary's parent problem was quite different. Lynn hesitated to invite her crowd to her home for a party because she was afraid of what they would think of her father. And Mary was sure that a very special boy was laughing at her mother's fantastic hats. Both were happily surprised by what happened. It never occurred to Peggy that her father could have any suggestions about how she could make friends in her new school. But when he had a plan for her, she was delighted that it worked.

Although the kind of life your mother had in her teens was different from yours, one part of it has not changed. She had the same dreams and hopes, and the same feelings as yours. Because this is so, she understands your perplexities and problems. When you, in turn, understand this, real help is yours for the asking.

Yes, understanding is a two-way thing.

HELEN FERRIS

Contents

Suddenly You're in Love

HILA COLMAN

TINA WAS in a state of feverish excitement as she hurriedly put the finishing touches to her hair and makeup. She could hear Chris Randall's car pulling into the driveway, and she wanted to get downstairs fast. This was their first real date and she couldn't abandon him to the deep-freeze treatment he was bound to get from her parents!

Lucky thing he didn't know the hideous time she'd had at the supper table when she'd announced she was going out with him.

"You're not going to start going out with Chris Randall," her mother had said, throwing meaningful looks at Tina's father.

"Why not?" Tina had asked indignantly.

"For one thing, he's too old for you," her mother said, "and for another I don't like him."

1

"Too old?" Tina could hear her voice getting shrill. "Nineteen, too old! Oh, my God!"

"You can please leave God out of this," Mr. Porter said tersely. "It would seem to me that a nineteen-year-old boy who's been away to college for a year would find a sixteen-year-old high school girl somewhat immature. Frankly, Tina, I'd be suspicious of just why he's so eager to have a date with you."

"Thank you so much." Tina tried to muster her dignity. "Perhaps, my dear father, it's because he finds me attractive."

Tina wanted to cry at the cool smile on her father's face.

"Perhaps he does, but I should think he would want someone more sophisticated. I don't like him either. I don't like a boy who doesn't look you straight in the eye when he says hello. I don't think he's a suitable companion for you."

"You don't have to like him," Tina had said wildly. "I like him, and I'm going out with him. He's picking me up here at eight o'clock tonight, and there's nothing you can do about it."

Her parents exchanged glances, and Tina stared at them both defiantly. "There's a great deal we can do about it," her father said quietly. "You're still a very young girl, and your mother and I would be remiss in our responsibility if we let you run around with any boy who asked you."

"But what's wrong with Chris? You haven't said anything specific about him. You have to say more than that you don't like him!" Tina was afraid her anger was going to flow over into tears, and she'd have to greet Chris with red eyes and a swollen nose.

Didn't they understand that this was the most important night in her entire life?

2

There was a streak of insanity about the whole thing to Tina—her mother and father sitting there eating their roast lamb and broccoli, discussing Chris as if he were just an ordinary person, just another boy who'd asked her for a date. *For eight days now, she'd been achingly praying for Chris to take her out.*

She had never felt this way before about anyone. And least of all Robbie Tanner, whom she'd been dating all winter and whose mother was her mother's best friend. It made her sick the way her folks were so effusive with Robbie: "Why don't you ask him over for dinner?" and "We have two tickets for a concert—why don't you and Robbie go?" They were always so cordial and so sweet with him, as if he were somebody special! What would they say if they knew he'd had a bottle in his car at the Christmas dance, and that he always wanted to go up to Mt. Tom to park . . . ? Why were parents so stupid and blind, thinking they knew all the answers!

She and Nancy had run into Chris together, the first day he was home from college. The high school wasn't out for the summer yet, and she and Nancy had stopped in for a Coke after school. It was a broiling hot day for early June, and neither one of them had wanted to leave the air-conditioned drugstore. And suddenly there was Chris, sitting down beside them.

"Well, how's the old town been getting along without me all year?" he said, addressing them both.

Tina and Nancy knew him only very slightly, the way people know each other in a not-too-large New England town. Chris hadn't gone to the public high with the rest of them, but to a nearby private prep school, and had never been a part of the local teen-age crowd.

He looks different from the rest of the boys, Tina thought

3

immediately, as he swung his legs from the stool next to hers. There was a different cut to his light sports jacket, to his slim, tapered slacks, to the way he held himself and to his air of easy confidence.

"What do you two do for excitement around here?" Chris had looked directly into Tina's blue eyes when he spoke.

"We don't," Tina told him, laughingly. "Maybe you have some bright ideas."

"Maybe I have." There was a world of meaning in Chris's eyes when he said that, and little shivers ran down Tina's spine. She wished Nancy hadn't been with her; she wished she'd been sitting there alone with Chris. . . .

Outside the girls had watched him pull away in his mother's low sports car. Everyone in Watertown knew that car—bright red, always in a hurry, and when it stopped it was usually in front of the country club, the beauty parlor or the most expensive shops. Tina and Nancy looked after it wistfully.

"I'd give anything to go out with him," Nancy sighed. "Do you think he'll ever call us?"

Tina had shaken her head. "No, silly, we're just high school kids to him." But that was not what her heart was saying. He's going to call me! One of these days the phone will ring, and it will be Chris. . . . I feel it, I know it, I could see it in his eyes. . . . He was looking at me, not at Nancy. It was as though she weren't there. . . .

Every afternoon thereafter Tina had stopped in for a Coke, praying, hoping Chris would be there. When she could, she went alone, even though Nancy was her best friend. And then suddenly one day Chris was there . . . *waiting for her!* His long legs were wound around the stool, his jacket carefully folded on the seat beside him.

The minute she came in, he caught her eye and re-

4

moved the jacket with a low bow. "I fought man and beast holding this seat for you, but it's worth it." She had smiled into his eyes, intensely moved by the small thoughtfulness of the cherry Coke he had waiting for her.

The next day he had two cherry Cokes lined up for her. "So you'll have to stay here twice as long," he had said, his eyes sweeping her with a look that left her limp. And then he'd asked her for the date for Saturday night.

Now Saturday was here, and the red car was parked in *her* driveway, and Chris Randall was downstairs waiting for her. . . . After all the painful discussion, her parents had agreed she couldn't break her date at the last minute. Frantically she'd promised them everything they had demanded, not to be home late, not to start making a "thing" of dating Chris. . . . She would have promised her whole life away for this one night. . . .

Coming downstairs, she could feel the iciness in the living room. Her father was sitting in his armchair reading the newspaper, and her mother was holding herself erect with that same unhappy look she wore when she had to put her hands into dirty dishwater. And poor Chris was gallantly trying to be social and keep a conversation going!

Quickly Tina came to his rescue. "Chris, I'm *so* glad to see you." She threw her cardigan around her shoulders and, hardly saying goodnight to her folks, she linked her arm in his and led him out the door.

Outside, the soft summer evening was slowly lighting up. "*Star light, star bright, first star I see tonight, I wish I may, I wish I might, have the wish I wish tonight. . . .*" Tina spoke softly, making her wish silently to herself. She had to be so careful, so terribly careful tonight. She'd never been out with a college boy, with a boy like Chris, and her silent prayer was to *know*. To be able to say the right thing,

5

to do the right thing. Her life depended on this night—her whole summer, everything was hanging in the balance. If Chris really liked her, if she made a hit . . .

Her parents were behind her now, way behind. Somehow or other she would handle them. She would make them see how much Chris meant to her. Besides they had nothing specific against him!

Here she was in the little red car, and Chris was sitting beside her. She wished everything at once. She wished that Nancy, the whole of Watertown High were lined up to see her, and she wished she and Chris were some place far away, some place where no one they knew could see them at all, and they'd be alone for days and days. . . .

"What do you say we ride around for a bit, and then we can go over to the Inn and dance? It's too early to go there yet."

"Sounds wonderful." Slowly, Tina let herself relax against the seat. She had never ridden in one of these low, open sports cars before, and she mustn't let Chris know she was the least bit afraid. But it was so open and low and close to the ground! Tina held on to the door arm with her right hand as Chris zoomed out of the driveway and onto the highway. It was like riding in one of the little cars on the shoot-the-shoots—marvelous, exciting, breathtaking and scary!

Chris turned down Main Street, and Tina could see the heads of everyone turn around to watch them whiz by; she stretched her legs down into the depths of the floorboards feeling gloriously like a Hollywood star passing through town.

Chris didn't talk much; he pulled her over so she was sitting close beside him, and then he headed out toward the beach. "Let's see how the lake looks—"

The moon was up now, and Chris pulled the car into the

empty parking place. The katydids were making a racket in the woods, but the lake was quiet and shimmering in the moonlight.

"It's lovely, isn't it?" Tina spoke softly.

"Not bad," Chris agreed. "Let's go down and see what the water's like."

At the water's edge Tina slipped off her pumps, glad that she wasn't wearing stockings, and Chris took off his shoes and socks and rolled up his slacks. They let the cool water lap around their legs. "Later this summer we can come swimming down here at night," Chris said, holding her hand tight in his own. "We're going to have us a good time this summer, you and I. . . ."

Tina turned her face to his, and their eyes held each other's in the pale moonlight. "I hope so," she murmured. Swiftly Chris had his arms around her, and he was kissing her on the mouth. Tina had never been kissed like this before, and her body trembled. She held Chris close to her. . . . *I love you, I love you,* her mind was saying, but she wasn't ready to say it out loud, not yet. . . .

They walked along the beach for a while, holding hands. Chris spoke about college, about his fraternity, the fun of living in the frat house. "We can do anything we want up there," he said. "No dumb rules like in the dorms."

Tina put down the pang of jealousy she felt. What kind of things would he want to do? But it was a long summer ahead, and by the end of summer, who knew? Maybe she and Chris would be going steady, maybe she'd be the one going up to visit him for college weekends. . . . Her mind was racing ahead, and she felt as if tonight the whole world had suddenly opened up before her, that she was moving from a dull, childish existence into a new, magnificent life of being in love with a *man*, of growing up, of turning into a woman!

7

The feeling grew as the evening progressed. After tidying herself up in the car, they went on to the Inn, a Saturday-night favorite for many of the young marrieds in town. There wasn't a soul there from the high school, and at first Tina felt uneasy and shy recognizing some of the older couples that she knew her parents didn't particularly like. But after sitting at a table with Chris, laughing and chatting, and then dancing in his arms to the divine music, nothing mattered except the tremendous excitement of being with Chris, of leaning across the table listening to his easy drawl, of laughing with him at the silly jokes they shared, of looking into his dark, brown eyes, of feeling his arms tighten around her suddenly on the dance floor—and, best of all, of talking about the wonderful things they would do together all summer.

Of course, in the back of her mind, she knew she was going to have difficulty with her parents. But they had better face the fact that they couldn't wrap her up in cotton, that she was growing up and there was nothing they could do to stop her.

It was two o'clock in the morning when Chris took her in his arms in front of her house and kissed her goodnight. He kissed her eyes and he kissed her lips. "I'll call you tomorrow, honey. I'm so glad I've found you. You don't know how I was dreading the summer in this town, but having you, it's all different."

"For me, too," Tina whispered.

She stood on the porch, watching Chris drive away. The moon was still bright and clear, and Tina felt as if she could have floated right up into it. Quietly she opened the front door of the dark house, slipped off her shoes and was about to tiptoe up the stairs to her room. "Tina!" The light had snapped on and her father was on the stair landing. His face and his voice were stern with anger. "You were supposed to come home early. Where were you?"

It was like floating in a beautiful private bubble and suddenly having a shotgun go off in your ear. How dare you talk to me like that, Tina wanted to shout, how dare you try to ruin my evening! "We were out dancing. I didn't know it was so late, Daddy," she said in a low voice.

"That's no excuse. I'd like to know where you were dancing at this hour! We'll discuss this tomorrow morning, but let me tell you right now, no more dating with that Chris Randall again, do you understand?"

"We'll discuss it in the morning," she answered tightly. And then Tina fled past her father on the stairs. She had to hold in her sobs until she was safe in her own room, in her own bed. She didn't brush her teeth, she didn't wash up—she could almost taste Chris's lips on her own, and she wanted it to be that way forever. Tina dropped her clothes in a small pile on the floor and crept into bed, and then the sobs came.

This couldn't be happening. . . . Somehow she'd figure a way—they *couldn't* take Chris away from her.

The next day was Sunday, and her parents were at the breakfast table when she came downstairs. Then the cross-examination began: where had they driven to, when did they get to the Inn, had she had anything to drink, how many did Chris drink, did she think the Inn a proper place for him to take her, did she see any other high school girls there?

"You're treating me like a baby!" Tina cried out in despair. "Why don't you ask me all these questions when I go out with Robbie? He takes a drink sometimes, too, and he's brought me home pretty late!"

"I'm sure Robbie is no angel," her mother said, "but we

9

know Robbie and we trust him, that makes all the difference."

"You see, we care about you, honey." Her father's face was unhappy behind his graveness. "We care about where you are and whom you're with. And sometimes it's hard to explain why one boy is acceptable and another one isn't. I have nothing against Chris, but we just don't think he's right for you. You'll have to take our word for it."

"And what if I don't?" Tina said.

"I'm afraid you don't have any choice. You simply won't be allowed to go out at all. We'll have to know exactly where you are and whom you're with." Her father's voice was firm, and Tina knew, with a hideous, searing pain, that she had lost.

"I don't care then. If I can't go out with Chris, I won't go with anyone. You've ruined my whole summer now anyway. . . ." This time she couldn't keep the sobs back, and the tears were streaming down her face as she fled from the room. What would she say to Chris when he called . . . how could parents be this way! It was worse than being in prison!

Later when she heard her mother knocking on her door, she couldn't bear to let her in.

"Tina, please try to understand!" Her mother's voice came to her helplessly. "We don't *enjoy* doing this."

"I know," Tina sobbed, "but please leave me alone." Why was it so hard for parents and a daughter to understand each other! She felt sorry for them, and she felt sorry for herself, but seeing Chris seemed more important than anything.

She thought she'd die waiting for him to call, and when Chris finally did, all she could say was that school still had one more week to go, and since she couldn't go out on a school night, he should phone her later in the week. By that time, she figured, she'd have thought of some way out.

She couldn't bear staying in her room; she couldn't bear staying in the house with those anxious eyes of her parents following her around. Determinedly she got up and washed her face, brushed her hair, and walked downstairs in her most dignified manner. "I've changed my mind. I'm going over to see Nancy. My best friend, Nancy O'Donnell, if that's all right with you," she said.

Her mother's eyes were hurt. "Tina, we're only trying to do what's best for you. Of course, you can go over to see Nancy."

Nancy was alone when Tina arrived, and the two girls made themselves comfortable on Nancy's back porch. Tina poured out her story, telling Nancy about the glorious time she had had the night before, and the horrible aftermath that ensued. "I can't tell them I'm in love," she said in despair when she finished. "I don't know what to do. You're so lucky, Nancy, your parents never bother you. They let you do what you want."

This was an old cry of Tina's. She had always been envious of Nancy's freedom. Even though Nancy was a couple of months younger than Tina, Nancy's parents never questioned her about anything and let her come and go as she pleased. "You've got to take care of yourself someday, so you may as well learn now," Nancy's mother was fond of saying, and Tina had quoted this so much in her own home, she was asked not to bring it up any more.

"We don't agree with Mrs. O'Donnell's ideas, and what she does is none of our concern," her parents said. "We have our own standards, and we don't believe girls just grow up by themselves."

Now Tina's dark blue eyes were thoughtful. "You'll have

to talk to Chris, Nancy. You'll have to tell him about my parents. Maybe he'll have some bright ideas. Call him up and see if he'll meet you down at the drugstore. I couldn't talk to him on the phone when he called, and I can't bear to have him think—" Tina's eyes brightened at the thought of action. "Will you, Nancy?"

Nancy shrugged her shoulders. "Sure, why not? I don't mind talking to Chris. Won't he think it funny, though, if I call him?"

"No, he knows you're my best friend. Just tell him you have something you want to talk to him about. Go ahead. I don't want to do it myself. I don't want him to feel frozen out, but he mustn't think I'm chasing him either."

Tina's heart was beating nervously as Nancy dialed the number, and she felt a sting of uneasiness at the caressing tone of Nancy's voice when she was talking to Chris. "Okay," Nancy said when she hung up, "he's meeting me in twenty minutes."

"That's fine." Tina hugged Nancy affectionately. "Between the two of you, you'll think of something. I know you will!"

It was sheer will power that kept Tina from biting all her nails waiting for Nancy to come back. She was in her own room now and Nancy was to come there directly after she left Chris. Nancy's face was glowing when she arrived, and the minute Tina closed the door to her bedroom behind them, Nancy burst forth. "He's a doll, he's really divine, Tina. . . ."

"What did he say? Has he got any helpful ideas?" Tina asked eagerly.

"He said he couldn't think of anything right now. But guess what? He asked me to go to the movies with him tonight. He said you couldn't because of tomorrow being school," she added hurriedly, "but I can."

12

Tina stared at her friend unbelievingly. "You're not going, are you?"

Nancy grasped her hand. "Why not? You can't go . . . he'll go with someone. It may as well be me! Tina, please don't be angry."

"I'm not angry." Tina spoke slowly. "I just feel as if someone were burying me before my body was quite cold."

"Don't say things like that," Nancy pleaded. "Please! It's not my fault that your parents are that way, and mine aren't. I'd be crazy not to take advantage of it, wouldn't I?"

"I guess so," Tina agreed bleakly. "No, its not your fault. Oh, why do I have to have parents like this!"

Tina was to make that cry again and again in the next few weeks. The inevitable had taken place: Nancy was dating Chris Randall, and Tina was living in an agony of alternating fury and despair. She couldn't really blame Nancy, she probably would have done the same herself, and yet she couldn't bear to see her. She didn't want to hear about what Nancy and Chris were doing; swimming, dancing, going to the movies, walking in the moonlight alone, just as she and Chris had done that one perfect night. *It should be me doing all those things*, she kept thinking.

The situation with her parents didn't help either. Tina realized her mother was almost as miserable as she about the way she was moping around the house, yet her mother's, or her father's, attempts to pull her out of it made her feel more forlorn than ever.

A few times Mrs. Porter urged her to have a party. "You haven't had a party in ages," she said, "and you could invite that new boy who moved into the old Harris house."

"I don't feel like having a party," Tina said sadly, determined to resist her mother's attempts to introduce her to the tall, gangly boy across the way who seemed to be

13

spending his summer reading science fiction and playing his clarinet.

The night her father brought her home a surprise, a darling pocket-size transistor radio, Tina cried her eyes out. She had hugged her father hard, and she loved the radio, but playing it alone in her room later, the knowledge of her parents' love and their unhappiness for her, made her feel the weight of her own helplessness almost more. Why couldn't they understand? How did they decide one boy was right and another one wrong . . . ?

The summer days went by—warm, brightly sunny, glorious days made for having fun . . . and each evening more perfect than the one that had gone before. There seemed to be a special softness in the air that summer, a special fragrance. Tina drank it in, sitting by her bedroom window gazing out into the evening sky. Life might stretch on endlessly this way for her, she mused.

She had made up her mind not to see Robbie at all. He kept calling her, and he dropped in every so often, but to Tina he was now a dull clod. And all her mother's persuasions were not going to change her mind. Now and then, Tina would notice the boy across the street. He'd swing lazily in the hammock with a pile of magazines on his chest (it was cute the way they went up and down without falling!) or he'd putter in front of the house on an ancient car of his. Sometimes staring out her window at night she'd see him outlined against the window as he practiced his clarinet. She could hear him, and she couldn't help noticing that he played well. Plaintive music—a little lonely—expressing in some strange, almost telepathic way, her present emotions. Once she even had the odd thought that she'd like to meet this new boy—something in his playing caught at her. But the next moment, she chided herself. It's Chris I want, her heart cried, and no one else will ever mean the same. Day and night she lived with the thought that Nancy, her best friend, was going out with Chris, having a whole summer that should have been hers. How could she comfort the hurt look in her parents' eyes when it was they who had brought all this about . . . ?

It was almost the end of July, a haunting, lazy evening. Tina was alone in the house, and when the phone rang she ran to answer it quickly.

It was Nancy. They chatted as they always did, and finally Nancy asked her what she was doing.

"Nothing, as usual," Tina said.

"Chris and I are just going riding around. Why don't you come with us?" Nancy asked impulsively. "We'll bring you home before your folks get out of the movies. Come on!"

Tina barely hesitated. "All right, I will." Surprised by her own courage, she flew upstairs to get herself ready. To see Chris . . . to fly out of her coop on an evening like this. . . . She had never done anything like this before in her life, and she hoped they would hurry and pick her up before she lost her nerve.

But this wasn't a real date with Chris . . . what harm could it be for the three of them to just go for a short ride?

She was waiting for them when the little red car pulled up, her heart beating excitedly at the thought of seeing Chris. Nancy made room for her in front, and with Chris's casual, good-natured banter, the three of them were in high spirits as Chris stepped on the gas.

"Shall we give Tina the Randall special?" Chris said to Nancy.

"What's that?" Tina asked.

Nancy giggled. "You'll find out. But hold tight, that's all I can say."

"I don't like tricks in a car," Tina said.

15

"Don't worry, nothing will happen to you," Chris confidently assured her.

They purred along the highway, and Tina felt marvelous. This was better than staying in her room alone. Why hadn't she thought of doing this before, instead of just moping? Mentally she took back the mean things she'd thought about Nancy.

"Well, here we go," Chris announced. They were headed back toward town—just on the outskirts. Chris started zooming in and out of the blocks, turning around the corners as close to the curb as he could get, and if there wasn't any curb he'd skirt a fence or a tree so close by the girls were howling.

"Chris, I'm getting seasick," Tina cried.

They turned a corner sharply, and suddenly there was a hideous tearing noise. Tina felt the car lurch out of control. She didn't know what was happening, but there was a fence crashing down, the pickets going in all directions like sticks in an earthquake—and then the car hit against a wall. Tina heard herself let out a cry, and she felt Nancy's hand gripping hers. Then suddenly all was still.

Tina looked wildly about. What they had hit was the side of a small building—something that looked like a playhouse—and they had demolished the whole side of the fence. She said, "Heaven help us—" And then, before she could utter another word, Chris snapped into almost hysterical action and was backing out of the lawn the car had jumped. She looked at him in stunned astonishment. "Aren't you even going to stop to see what you did? We should investigate—"

"What good will that be?" Chris asked. "To heck with it, they'll never know who did it."

"That's awful," Nancy said. "You should stop."

16

"You certainly should," Tina agreed. "Chris, go on back!"

"You're chicken, both of you. Why should I stop just to get into some trouble?"

The three of them were silent as Chris kept racing the car on, and all three of them jumped when a long, clear, unmistakable siren sounded close. In the next moment the police car was beside them, edging them over to the side of the road.

"What do you think you're doing, young man?" Tina recognized the familiar face of one of the local policemen, his ruddy face stern with anger. "Speeding, destroying property and running away, driving like a maniac. . . . We don't think much of hit-and-run drivers. Let's see your license."

Chris's hand was trembling as he pulled his license out of his wallet. "I didn't mean any harm," he mumbled, "my mother'll take care of the damage. . . ."

The policeman looked at him contemptuously. "Maybe it'd be a better idea if you took care of it. Come on, I'm going to take you back to see Judge Davis. You follow me back to the courthouse. Your girl friends can let their folks take them home. Follow me, and no tricks."

Nancy and Tina kept close together as they followed Chris and the officer up the courthouse steps. "This had to happen tonight!" Tina whispered to Nancy. "My folks are going to kill me. . . . I'm so scared and nervous!"

"Me too," Nancy said hopelessly.

Chris disappeared into a back room with the police officer, and the two girls called home. Then, pale-faced and nervous, they waited for their parents to arrive. Tina didn't know where to begin her explanations. "What are you going to say?" she asked Nancy anxiously.

17

"Say?" Nancy seemed preoccupied. "I don't know what I'll say. . . . I'll . . ." There were tears in her eyes as she turned to Tina, and then abruptly she burst into sobs. "They're not even coming for me," she cried wildly, burying her face against Tina and sobbing uncontrollably. "My mother *laughed* on the phone—she thought it was a huge joke. . . . They're having a party at my house, and she said your father would bring me home. Oh, Tina, you're so lucky!"

Nancy's sobs burst from her as if they had been imprisoned for years. She buried her head in Tina's lap and cried so that her whole body was shaking. Tina felt as if she wanted to cry with her. Every nerve in her body seemed to be involved, and Tina felt choked with emotions that were tearing her apart. She thought of the tremendous concern in her own mother's voice on the phone . . . just the question, "Darling, are you all right? We'll be there right away!" She couldn't digest it all—for years she'd known that her parents and Nancy's were different, yet she had never really known at all *how* different!

"They care about you," she said comfortingly to Nancy, trying to convince herself. "They're just different. . . ."

"I'll say." Nancy was trying to quiet her deep gasps. "You don't know what it's like, feeling that no one gives a darn when you get home or even if you do get home, who you see, where you are. . . . You think you have a hard time, but you don't know how awful *this* is. . . . And Chris really is kind of a punk, but my folks wouldn't care, they wouldn't even bother to know him. . . . You saw how he acted tonight."

"Yes, I know . . ." Tina hadn't wanted to think about Chris. How could her parents have known? She was silent as waves of conflict rocked through her.

And suddenly her parents were there. A warm, tender

relief flooded her as they took her in their arms. "Are you all right?" her mother asked again and again.

"Oh, Mom," was all Tina could say, feeling the wondrous, familiar closeness of her parents' arms encircling her. She was incredulous at herself for having forgotten all summer that this love existed and was hers. "Oh, Mom," she repeated.

After they dropped Nancy home, Tina sat between her parents silently. This was a night to remember, and when they reached their own driveway, Tina stayed outside alone in the soft, summer moonlight. The sweet, lonely note of a clarinet in the opposite house broke the stillness, and Tina's heart responded with a quickened beat. It had been a lonely summer—a sad summer. . . . Thinking now of Chris and his cowardice, his shallowness, she realized it had also been a wasted summer. But it was only half over. . . . With a shy smile in the darkness, she waved silently to the boy's figure silhouetted at the window. . . . Yes, tomorrow was another day.

Easter Present

RITA C. FOSTER

CARRYING my books and the bundle, I shut the front door behind me, and then stood on the porch for a minute, sort of feeling the morning. It was lovely—cool, but beginning to warm up for spring, and the little soft lonesome wind out of the south that simply calls to me, and the sky so blue you could hardly believe it. I love spring, and I love Easter, and I was in love with this day, only I had to go to school, and there were things at home that I needed to keep an eye on. Mother had been talking of buying a new hat.

She wasn't getting it just for Easter; she thinks Easter is a time to redecorate your heart, and that putting on new clothes is a poor substitute for inside spring cleaning. But she has sort of original ideas for hats for her age, if you understand me, and I always try to go along when she shops for them. Otherwise, she is apt to get something that looks as if it had a sample of every kind of flower that blooms in the parks, and a feather from most of the birds.

I'll never forget Easter last year. Mother and I were just coming out of church when Bill—that's a boy down the street—drove by in his Crosley, and looked at Mother and almost ran up on the curb. She was wearing a new hat, not nearly as bad as some she gets, but it was pretty striking, I guess, if you weren't used to them. This particular one was a blue sailor, but it had pink roses all over it, but *all* over it.

The next day Bill said to me, "I saw you and your mother yesterday, Mary," and then laughed and laughed. I just couldn't stand another incident like that, and I couldn't hurt Mother's feelings by telling her what kind of hat to buy. The only thing I could think of to do was to fix this hat over—that's why I had it with me today—and tell her it was an Easter gift. She wouldn't hurt my feelings by not wearing it, and I felt I could make a fairly good-looking hat out of it.

Anyway, school was waiting for me, so I started out. The robins were making an awful to-do, and some bluejays were scolding each other. I started down the walk, and hoped I wouldn't be too late to pick up Alicia.

Alicia and her mother have just recently moved here, although in a way it is a sort of homecoming for them. Alicia's father lived here years ago, and when he died Mrs. Mason decided to come back, because they didn't have a home anywhere else. Alicia is awfully smart—I mean fashion-smart, not school-smart—and her mother is, too. Not pretty, but slim and dark, rather exotic-looking, and with that assured manner that living in big cities gives a woman. She is very different from Mother in looks. Although I love Mother's nice skin and blue eyes, and her

22

hair that is still so soft and bright, yet I must admit she hasn't much figure left.

I wasn't too late for Alicia. She came down the steps just as I turned her corner, and saw me and waited for me. Lots of times we didn't talk much. I sometimes had the feeling she wanted to tell me something, but just couldn't bear to say it, so of course I never asked her about it.

"I wish I didn't have to go to school today," I said. "I'd like to get the Easter eggs ready."

She was so surprised she almost stopped. "Easter eggs?" she said. "You don't mean to tell me you play with Easter eggs? At your age?"

It was my turn to be surprised. "Why, Easter wouldn't be Easter without eggs. Yes, and baked ham for dinner, and angel food cake."

She didn't say anything for a minute, and I thought over what I had just said. It was true, and yet how could you make anybody see or feel what things like that meant to you? Easter eggs, now—there were all the years when I was little, and had gone out early Easter morning to look for them. Our lawn is of bluegrass, and it always gets green very early. So whenever I thought of colored eggs I could see and feel the short, soft, bright grass and smell the fragrance of it in the spring morning.

Alicia seemed to be getting ready to say something. Finally it came out, sort of slow and hurt. "I never did do anything special on Easter. Except get new clothes. Mother always sees to it, of course, that we're outfitted properly. Otherwise we never do anything unusual. She says it's just a survival of pagan customs."

"I s'pose so," I agreed. I knew there was more to it than that, though. After all, it's not easy to say that you know that there has always, since there were men in the world, been a holy day in the spring, when they were fairly certain

23

they weren't going to starve to death for another year; but still it means to you—well, a shining clean house, and colored eggs, and flowers, and a new year beginning, and a general feeling of being risen from the old worn-out dead things that you are through with now.

Spring flowers—forget-me-nots, and hyacinths, and roses, and daisies—"Oh, gee," I said.

"What is it now?" Alicia jumped.

"I just remembered about my mother," I said. "I'm afraid she's buying a new hat today. So I have to get some daisies at the dime store."

"Don't you want her to have a new hat?" she asked.

"Well, in a word, no," I said. "If I'm not with her, she gets something that is just an enormous bunch of flowers and feathers and veil. And this year's style will be fatal. She's always so happy about spring that it goes to her head, I guess—and I don't mean that for a pun, either. Anyway, I'm going to trim one for her this time, so she won't need a new one.

"I'm not going to do too much to it," I continued. I wasn't too sure of my own ability, to tell the truth. "I'm going to take all the roses off, and put a row of daisies, flat around the brim. It's navy blue, so I think it ought to look pretty good."

Even at school I still had the things at home on my mind. Mother loved flowers so much, and what she called "sweet" hats, and really what she wore didn't hurt anybody else. But I simply couldn't stand having her laughed at.

After lunch, I got a few of the other girls from the glee club together, and we went off to one of the music class-rooms and sang some Easter songs, the ones we could manage. We tried the *Hallelujah Chorus* finally, but didn't get very far with it, and then the bell rang. "Gee, but I love that thing," I said to Alicia as we went down the hall.

"Me, too," she said, and waited a minute and then went on very quickly, "Look, I just got a new record of it. Why don't you come down to my house this afternoon and hear it?"

It was the first time she had ever asked me to her house. I said, "Sure, I guess I can go for a little while. I've got some Easter records, too. Maybe you can come down and hear mine tomorrow."

In the afternoon I worked on Mother's hat in sewing class, and it turned out even better than I had hoped. It would never look like one of Mrs. Mason's hats, because it had too many flowers. But then, if it didn't have some flowers, Mother would be too disappointed; and it had lots less than she generally wore.

After school we started out for Alicia's house, but as we got close to it her face got a set, hurt look and I knew she was trying to think how to say something, and it must be something not very pleasant. Finally she wet her lips and said, "Mary, does your mother love you?"

I thought it was an awfully silly question, but she seemed to mean it seriously, so I just said, "Why, yes. Sure."

"I don't mean that way," she said. "I mean, does she *really* love you—would she love you even if you weren't any relation to her?"

I couldn't possibly imagine, under any circumstances, not being any relation to Mother, but I tried. And finally I said, "Yes, I believe she really loves me, but with Mother you can't break it away from being her daughter; she loves me anyway, but she loves me especially because I am hers."

Alicia nodded her head a little bit, as if that was what she had thought all the time. "Well," she said finally, "my mother doesn't really love me at all."

"That's just plain silly," I told her. "Everybody loves their own children."

"Just because you have a completely perfect home and mother," Alicia turned on me furiously, "doesn't mean that everybody else has. And it doesn't mean that you know everything about everybody else either." I could see that she was almost crying. "She may sort of like me, but I know she doesn't love me, not really. She practically told me so once when we saw you and your mother on the street. You were laughing together, and holding hands. . . . That's why she buys me more clothes than I need, and gives me so much allowance."

I just couldn't make myself believe it. Mrs. Mason's fine, delicate features came up in my memory and I felt that anybody with a face like that was sure to do the right thing—the correct, kind, agreeable thing—all the time. Alicia must just be having a spell of nerves.

"I don't really believe you," I said, "but of course you're entitled to your own opinion. Especially about your own mother." I tried to make it sound very sarcastic and disapproving, so that she would be forced into a kind of family loyalty.

"I know you think I'm terrible—" she wouldn't even look at me— "but it's true. Nobody is sorrier than I am about it. If you don't believe me, just watch her. It's the first time you've been at our house, and you'll notice."

When we reached the house and went in, Mrs. Mason had just come in, too.

She smiled a little at me and said, "Hello," in her light, clear voice, and I was farther than ever from believing what Alicia had said. We all went into the living room, Mrs. Mason looking over the mail. "More Easter cards," she said. "Well, cards are all right, I suppose, but really it's almost disgusting, the effort being made to commercialize

Easter. Give flowers, give perfumes, give handkerchiefs, give blouses. . . . Really, I can't see why I should give anything to anybody else just because it is Easter."

"That's what my mother and I think, too," I agreed. "Some of the people we know are beginning to give small gifts, but my mother just sends around a few Easter eggs, or potted flowers, to the people she loves most."

"Well, I certainly hope no one sends me anything," Mrs. Mason said, rather irritably. "I know of no one to whom I feel an urge to give a present."

The Masons' house is older than ours and doesn't have so many windows; but even at that it didn't seem that the room needed to be as dark as it was. Partly, I guess, it was the walls. They were a sort of dark tan, and the curtains were cream colored; or maybe it was just that they hadn't been washed for some time. There was dust on everything, too. I felt that Mrs. Mason probably didn't get much fun out of housekeeping, and didn't care too much for her home. In fact, while I still couldn't believe what Alicia had said, I felt all at once that Mrs. Mason didn't care much for anything except herself.

Still I didn't want her to feel embarrassed about the way the house looked, so I said, "I can only stay a little while, I've got to get home and help. We haven't quite got all our housecleaning done either." But it *was* almost finished, all spic and span and shining; the floors and windows and mirrors were polished, the curtains were crisp and fresh, even my shelves of little glass animals had been washed.

Mrs. Mason just looked around and said indifferently, "Oh, I haven't started spring cleaning yet. I don't know that I shall do much this year, anyway. In these days one keeps a house pretty well cleaned as one goes along. Periodical housecleaning, I always think, belonged to the old days before vacuum cleaners and our other modern housekeeping aids." However, it didn't look as if she used many of those aids, or at least not regularly.

But Mother often says something of the sort, and I agreed. "I expect you're right," I said, "but my mother always says that at Easter her house is going to look extra bright and shining."

She said, "Oh, really?" and raised her eyebrows at me for a moment, and then laid the mail and her bag and gloves on a table. Then she went and raised some of the shades a little, and straightened a chair. It was as if she found me and my ideas not interesting, and had dismissed me. Alicia wasn't saying anything at all, just putting the record on the machine.

Mrs. Mason turned around after raising the shades, and I got a really good look at her, the closest to her I had ever been. She didn't actually look as I had thought she did; and her hair wasn't brushed silky, it was just oily. Under the shiny, small black hat her fine features looked sharp, her mouth was rather tight, and her eyes snapping.

I hardly knew whether to try to continue the conversation with her or go over to Alicia, but Mrs. Mason turned back to me. "I suppose you do go to church on Easter? I must finish my shopping tomorrow. I haven't been able to find the exact shade in gloves to match my suit, and I want Alicia to give her opinion about a scarf." When she said Alicia's name she didn't smile at her, as Mother almost always does at me when she talks about me while I am in the room.

"We don't go in much for Easter outfits," I said grimly. I suppose I had better not have started this at all, I thought, but since I had already told her so much of our customs I would go on. "We always have clothes suitable to the season, and as nice as we can afford, but we don't feel that we have to always have new things. But—" and I giggled a little, it seemed such a come-down, "we always do have a special Easter dinner. Ham, and angel food cake, and scalloped potatoes, and strawberries, if we can find them."

"Indeed?" Mrs. Mason had completely lost interest in me, and didn't bother to hide it. "It's a new idea, to celebrate Easter by cleaning house and stuffing oneself."

Alicia had finally got the record on and started, and now the great chorus began to fill the room. To me it always seems to be framed in gold and scented with lilies, and it almost hypnotizes me, but it didn't affect Mrs. Mason that way. She put her hands quickly to her temples, and said, in a tone that burned and stabbed and dripped icicles all at once—a tone I have never heard used in my home in my life—"Alicia! I have asked you never to play those noisy, emotional things while I am at home! Turn it off instantly!"

Alicia, her back to me, turned it off quickly, and then started for the hall door. I knew she was going to her room to cry, so I started out too, and I said, "Don't mind, Alicia. Bring it down to my house tomorrow and we'll play it then. My mother loves it. Yes, and she loves Easter, too."

As I started toward home, I didn't even notice at first how slowly I was walking. How awful—how perfectly awful, a home like that! A messy house, a mother who didn't like her home or her daughter, no father that you knew you could always depend on, no jokes and fun and laughing, no fixing for family celebrations—nothing but clothes and some money! Why, after all, what real difference did it make what Mother wore? I began to be very doubtful about what I was carrying in the bundle.

Just then somebody came up from behind me, and Bill said, "Hello. Taking your Easter bonnet home?"

I almost jumped, I had been so busy thinking, but I said, "Oh, no, just something for my mother."

He said, "I'll bet it's her Easter bonnet, then. Say, is it anything like that one she was wearing last Easter?" and he began to grin.

"Could be," I said. "What's so funny?"

"I guess I never got around to telling you." He looked down at me, still smiling. "Once when I was a kid I had been at Grandmother's, and she sent a great big bunch of pink roses home to my mother. On the way a couple of bees began buzzing around me, and then some of the kids in my gang saw me, and started picking on me. I couldn't put the flowers down or the guys would have torn them up, and I couldn't hang on to them or the bees would sting me. I'd forgotten about that time until I saw your mother's hat last Easter. Then when I saw the roses—it struck me how funny it all was. . . ."

I said, not looking at him, "This one has daisies." So he hadn't been laughing at Mother's hat at all!

"Oh, well, daisies are nice, too."

Then he turned off at his street.

I started to hurry. Alicia had said I had a perfect home and mother. That was true, and all the things I had said to her were true, too; Mother did love Easter, and girls, and music, and my father, and her church and our neighbors—practically everybody, and that of course must be why everybody loved her. I began to feel all over Easterish, happy, and well, just Hallelujah! And all at once I wanted to see my mother—right away.

First, though, I had something to do. I turned and ran back to Mrs. Andrews' apartment, and gave the hat to her maid. She thought it was lovely and was so happy it made me feel even better.

Then I could face Mother with a clear conscience, and know I really didn't care at all what kind of hat she had, that it was just Mother herself, sweet and kind and generous, who mattered. And I walked faster and faster; I did want to get home.

As I came in sight of our little white house, the light from the living room was shining out the picture window, and I could see that Mother had had her annual Easter fling, for a great white lily was sitting on the table in front of the window. She always felt she should share it with everyone who went by. I quickly ran up the steps, and as soon as I got the door open I knew she was there, because there was a light and good smells coming from the kitchen.

She put her head around the door frame and called hello to me. I guess she hadn't been home long, for she still had something on her head. I seemed to have some water in my eyes—the afternoon air had been chilly—but I could tell it was pink, with shades of blue and white and green, and around it sort of a yellow glow, and I said, "Gee, your new hat is sweet. Looks just like a halo on you."

New Girl in Town

ROBERT PATERSON

OVER THE TOP of his newspaper, Sam Porter glanced uneasily toward the kitchen from which came the low-tense murmur of his fifteen-year-old daughter Peggy talking to her brother Billy as they cleaned up the supper dishes.

"It's my turn now—and they can *crawl*—" The rest was lost to Sam, but the tone was unmistakable.

"Aw, you're nuts!" came Billy's high, young voice.

"Well, I mean it!" said Peggy. "They can crawl!"

Sam frowned. Was this the same daughter who not two months ago stood before him in an agony of loneliness and confusion?

"They don't *like* me!" she had whispered, tears welling from the blue eyes so like her mother's. "Am I a *creep* or something?" Sam had put his arms around her. "It isn't that they dislike you, honey. But they've lived in this town all their lives. They've grown up with their friends. And you're new. They'll get to know you, and then they'll love you as much as we do."

"But I've been here two whole weeks and they don't even seem to *want* to know me!" And then the sobs had come and, holding her, Sam himself had never felt more lonely or inadequate. Helen would have known what to do. But Helen was gone. And he was a widower. And he and Peggy and Billy were alone in this world except for one another. It had been tough enough in their own town. But at the beginning of the year the printing company he worked for had transferred him here to Birchwood, where they were strangers.

"We'll think of something, honey," he'd said with an assurance he had not felt. "Don't you worry."

Now he heard the kitchen-cupboard doors slam, and quickly busied himself with the newspaper.

"Hi, Daddy," Peggy said from the living-room doorway. "Anything in the paper tonight?"

Sam forced a grin as he looked up at her. "You got a mention in Bill Dillon's column today. By the way," he added, "how are you getting along with the kids at school?"

She met his gaze for a moment, then shrugged. "They're no problem."

Sam let the newspaper slip to the floor. It had been a long, hard pull, and now it looked as if it had been wasted. That first night, when Peggy had cried out her bitterness to him, he had lain awake in bed a long time, his mind searching for a way to ease her hurt. By breakfast next morning, he at least had a question.

"Peggy," he had said, buttering a piece of toast, "what do you do best?"

Billy's grin flashed over his glass of milk. "Sleep in, maybe? She sure can do that!"

"No, I'm serious," Sam continued. "Is there any one thing you excel in?"

Peggy frowned at her plate and hunched her shoulders. "Why do you ask?"

Sam smiled. "Honey, I did a lot of thinking last night. Maybe I have an answer."

She eyed him dubiously.

"If there's something you can do really well—be the best at, I mean—it could be the key you're looking for."

"But what?"

Sam spread his hands. "I know you're a good swimmer. Do you suppose you could become a good enough swimmer to be a credit to your school?"

Peggy said slowly, "Our school doesn't even have a tank."

"There's one downtown at the community center."

"I know. But nobody goes there."

"All the better," Sam said. "Then nobody will know."

"Know what?" Peggy shook her head dolefully. "I just don't understand, Daddy," she said. Her glance went to the clock. "I'm going to be late for school if I don't get out of here pretty soon."

Sam put a hand on her shoulder. "All right, honey. But you think about this swimming business. And don't say anything to anyone."

Peggy gave a brief, mirthless laugh. "That should be easy."

At noon that day, Sam went to the office of the Birchwood *Herald*, the small daily newspaper that served the area. There was a tall, dark-haired girl behind a counter. "Do you have back issues that I could look through?" he inquired.

"Surely," the girl said, smiling. "All we ask is that you don't clip the files."

35

Within half an hour Sam had all the evidence he wanted. During the past four years Birchwood High had not had a winner in the interschool swimming meet, open to all high schools in the country. For the past two years Birchwood had not even shown an entry.

That night after supper, Sam called Peggy into the living room and told her what he had discovered. "I'll tell you something else I did. I went down to the community center and talked to a man named Balsom. He's a swimming instructor, and he's interested."

"But, Daddy—" there was concern in Peggy's eyes— "you didn't tell him about the kids, or anything?"

Sam smiled reassuringly. "Of course not, honey. I just told him you were interested in training for the next high school meet, but that you didn't want anyone to know about it in case it didn't work out. He understood."

Peggy stared thoughtfully at the fireplace for a moment, and he could see that the tears were not far away. "Gee, I don't know, Daddy."

"Honey, if it doesn't work, you won't be any worse off than you are right now. And nobody'll know. So how about giving it a try?"

She looked at him, and he patted her hand. "OK," she said in a small, uncertain voice. "When do I go?"

On Monday of the last week in February there was a story in the *Herald* announcing that the interschool swimming meet had been scheduled for the first Saturday in March. Sam read it to Peggy and Billy. And next day Mr. Balsom called Sam on the telephone.

"I've had a talk with George French, head of physical education at Birchwood High," he began. "And—"

"Did you tell him what was going on?" Sam interrupted.

36

"I had to. If Peggy's going to be entered in this meet, George French has to do it."

"Of course," Sam admitted apologetically. "I'm afraid I hadn't really thought of that. What do you think of her chances?"

"She's a good swimmer, Mr. Porter. She does very well in practice. But then swimming in competition is a different thing entirely." Balsom paused. "There's a girl who swims for Roselawn. Marie Phillips. She won both the backstroke and the freestyle last year and the year before. Her coach is Mark Hanford, and he's one of the best in the state."

Sam took a deep breath. "You mean Peggy doesn't have much of a chance?"

"In a race, everybody has a chance. But there's no point in kidding ourselves. If Peggy beats Marie Phillips, it will be an upset."

Sam stared at his desk, trying not to feel let down. "I see," he said finally. "Well, thanks very much anyway, Mr. Balsom. I'm sure—"

"Just a minute!" Balsom cut in. "There's one other important factor."

"What is that?"

"Surprise," said Balsom. "Marie Phillips has been in a class by herself in school meets almost since she started swimming. She'll probably come into this one thinking it's a breeze. And the shock may turn the trick for us. But don't say anything about this to Peggy. I don't want her to be thinking about anything except getting from one end of the pool to the other as fast as she can."

"OK, Mr. Balsom," Sam agreed.

It was at supper on Tuesday of the following week that Sam noticed something seemed to be wrong with Peggy.

Lately she had become almost her old happy self, full of laughter and interested in everything that was going on. But tonight she appeared listless and preoccupied.

They were doing the dishes, and Billy was upstairs with his homework when Peggy paused in the middle of putting a dish into the cupboard.

"It's out of the bag, Daddy," she said. She picked another dish out of the drainer and began to wipe it dry. "I saw it myself on the bulletin board at school. The entries for the swimming meet!" There was anguish in her eyes. "What am I going to do?"

"Why, nothing, of course, honey."

"But everybody'll know!"

"I wouldn't worry, Peggy." Sam put his arm around her. "Cheer up. In a week it'll all be over. And then the kids will all be on your side. They'll be for you, not against you. Wait and see."

"But what if I come in last in every race?"

"Go on—" Sam chuckled, giving her a playful slap— "get those dishes finished. You won't come in last. Not if you swim as hard as you can. As a matter of fact, I have it straight from your trainer—but don't tell him I told you— that if you really put out, you might even come in first."

Peggy stopped in the center of the kitchen floor, a half-dried dish in her hand, disbelief in her eyes. "Did Mr. Balsom really say that?"

Sam nodded. "If you do your best."

At twenty minutes to one on the first Saturday in March, Sam and Billy climbed the long stairs leading up to the gallery that overlooked the pool at Williams Collegiate. Together they pushed their way through the glass doors, and immediately the air was warm and moist, smelling faintly of chlorine. They took seats near the rail. Below them, the water was clear and clean, the surface slightly choppy. They had been given a program and now Sam examined it. The juniors came first, then the intermediates, and finally the senior races.

"Mr. Porter?"

Sam turned. Coming along the row toward their seats was a short, blond young man in dark slacks and a white shirt with Birchwood High crest on the pocket. He smiled as he approached, and Sam stood up.

"I'm George French. Mind if I sit down?"

"Not at all," Sam said. "I suppose you already know Billy."

"Sure do." The teacher ruffled Billy's hair. "I just wanted to tell you how glad we are that your daughter is swimming for the school. It's been a long time since we had anything going for us in this meet. Too long."

"So I understand," Sam acknowledged.

"To be perfectly frank," the teacher went on, "I hope, of course, that Peggy will do well enough to satisfy herself, so that she'll want to continue. But I also hope that whatever success she has will help encourage others to take up competitive swimming."

"It could be a good thing," Sam agreed.

"As you can imagine, with no tank at school, we have a problem. But it isn't one that can't be solved—especially if we can build up interest and enthusiasm."

Sam eyed the teacher for a moment. "What do you think of Peggy's chances?"

"Fair enough," Mr. French said. "Of course her chances in the intermediate class are far better than they are in the senior."

"Senior?" Sam stared. "How many events has she entered?"

"Didn't she tell you? She's entered the freestyle and

39

backstroke events in both intermediate and senior classes. It was her own idea. I would have been quite satisfied with intermediate, myself. Because then, of course, she wouldn't have had to swim against Marie Phillips. But she was all for it. And she's a very determined girl, Mr. Porter."

"Well, what do you know!" Sam said. "What time is her first race?"

Mr. French took a small card from his pocket. "They ran the junior events off this morning. This afternoon it's all girls. They'll start with the intermediate backstroke, followed by the breaststroke, freestyle and relay, in that order. Then they'll repeat on the senior. Tonight they'll have the boys' events." He glanced up at the clock on the wall at the end of the gallery. "I'd better go down now. They should be coming out for a warmup pretty soon." He held up crossed fingers, and grinned. "See you later."

"How many races will Peggy have to swim in, Dad?" Billy asked, peering over the railing to where a group of swimmers was clustered around a bench at one end of the pool. "I don't see her anywhere."

Sam looked around. While he and George French had been talking, the gallery had almost filled. School kids, mostly, with colored pennants and equally colorful clothes. But quite a sprinkling of adults. He was surprised to see a group of youngsters make their way to the small section reserved for Birchwood rooters. They were nice-looking kids, and they certainly were adding their share to the rising level of noise. He only hoped they had come to cheer and not to scoff.

"Four," he said in response to Billy's question. "She'll be in the first race, and—"

"There she is!" Billy pointed. "Look!"

Sam leaned forward and, sure enough, there she was coming from the entrance toward one of the benches at

40

the end of the pool. She was wearing a white bathing cap, and a white robe with a big letter B on it. She was followed by George French, and a young woman Sam didn't recognize. Sudden tears burned in the back of his eyes. She was so alone down there. So very much alone! He saw the teacher pointing up to where they sat, and he leaned over and waved and she waved back. "Atta girl, honey!" he shouted.

The pool had been marked off into five lanes, and in each lane swimmers were having a brief warmup. Sam watched as Peggy slipped off her robe and went over to wait for one of the lanes to clear.

"Yea . . . *Birchwood!*"

Sam glanced over to where the Birchwood youngsters were sitting. They had seen Peggy, and now their cry went up, and Sam was grateful. But his gratitude turned suddenly to dismay as their yell was followed by a burst of laughter.

"What a hope!" one of them shouted, and immediately there was more laughter.

"Ah, shut your big fat mouth!" Billy screamed. "If you're so good, why aren't you in there swimming? I ought to come over and—"

"Billy!" Sam grabbed his son. "Sit down and be quiet. I know how you feel, but you won't help Peggy by antagonizing them."

Quickly he looked back down at the pool. He'd missed Peggy's dive. But there she was, stroking smoothly along. He hadn't seen her swim since their vacation in August last year. Now she swam higher out of the water and, although her stroke seemed almost leisurely, she appeared to be moving much faster. When she reached the end of the pool, she executed a little sort of flip turn and then was on her way back down the lane.

41

"Excuse me, Mr. Porter."

Sam glanced up. "Hello," he said to John Balsom. He introduced the swimming instructor to Billy, and then all three sat down.

"Quite a change in Peggy's swimming, Mr. Balsom," Sam commented.

"She's a pleasure to work with, Mr. Porter," Balsom said. "Beautiful coordination and amazing stamina."

Sam turned to him, pleased. "We lived on a river before we came here, and so she has just about grown up in the water." He shook his head. "But I can't get over the change in her style."

Balsom smiled. "It was easy. In fact, you may see one more radical change in Peggy's style before this meet is over."

Sam eyed him. "How do you mean?"

"Well, back in 1956, at Yale, they started teaching—" He broke off as a voice came out of the loud-speaker and the noise in the gallery ceased abruptly.

"First race of the afternoon program—intermediate backstroke. Girls, will you please take your places. Lane one—Haacke, Pulverston; lane two—McBride, of Roselawn; lane three—Janisse, of Harding; lane four—Simpson, of Collingsford; and lane five—Porter, Birchwood."

Throughout the announcement, a roar had shaken the air as each school was named—until the announcer reached Birchwood. Then came the cry that by now was familar to Sam.

"Yea . . . Birchwood! What a hope!" followed by laughter.

"Aw, shut up, you stupid mudheads!" Again Sam had to grab Billy, and the whole crowd laughed.

"Billy, for Pete's sake, watch the race and be quiet!"
Crack!

The water seemed filled with churning bodies and the air with noise as the contestants flung themselves backward down the pool. Sam had eyes for no one but Peggy, who was swimming second, behind Haacke of Pulverston.

"Come on, Peggy!" he yelled. He felt Balsom's hand on his arm.

"On the turn . . . on the turn," the swimming instructor was muttering, as the girls approached the end of the pool. "Ready . . . ready . . . *now!*"

Almost on the word, the two touched the end of the pool. For a split second the water churned in Peggy's lane and her feet flashed white, and then she broke surface on the return trip, stroking easily and a length in front.

"She's got it made," Balsom said quietly. And he was right. Peggy was waiting, one hand on the overflow, when the others began touching in. There was mild clapping from the gallery, and one small "Yea, Birchwood!"

Billy's face was screwed into a deep scowl as he glared across at the Birchwood section. "Yea, *Peggy!*" he corrected them.

Sam couldn't help grinning. "She's pretty good, isn't she?"

Balsom smiled. "Good enough to beat the intermediates, anyway."

It seemed only a minute or two before the breast-stroke event was over and then Peggy was back on the edge of the pool awaiting the starter's gun in the free-style race.

This time Peggy was in the center lane. She hit the water smoothly and, watching her, Sam did not see the girl in lane two slip and hit the water off balance. Peggy was just breaking surface, getting into her rhythm, when the other girl collided with her legs. There was a cry from the crowd, and Sam went to his feet, shouting.

"Don't worry," Balsom said quietly. "She's OK."

43

Halfway down the pool, Peggy was swimming fourth. She was third approaching the end of the tank. Sam saw again the quick churn, the flash of white feet, and once again Peggy was stroking leisurely and easily. She won it by an arm's length, and only then did Sam sit down.

Again came the voice of the loud-speaker: "The winner— Porter, of Birchwood." And then the polite handclapping and then "Yea . . . Birchwood!" But this time there was no laughter.

"Let's go down and see her," Sam said. "Want to go, Billy?"

Billy shook his head. "I want to watch the relay race."

Together, Sam and the swimming instructor made their way along the aisle to the glass doors, and then down the stairs. When they reached the first floor, Balsom led Sam along a broad corridor, their footsteps echoing noisily. "There's an anteroom just outside the girls' dressing room, and that's where they'll probably be," Balsom said as they stopped before a big door. He knocked, and a woman opened it a few inches. From inside came the chatter of excited voices.

"Is George French there with Peggy Porter?" Balsom asked. "This is Peggy's father."

The woman, still holding the door almost closed, shouted over her shoulder, "Mr. French?"

Immediately George French appeared. "Hello," he greeted them. "Want to come in for a minute?"

"If it wouldn't disturb anything," Sam said.

"She's resting," French told them. "But come on in. That freestyle was a close one, eh?"

The room was warm. Peggy sat on a plain wooden bench and sucked half a lemon, and Sam's mouth puckered involuntarily. "Well!" he exclaimed. "Congratulations!"

Peggy smiled and said, "Did I do all right, Daddy?"

Sam could only look at her. "Honey, you were wonderful." He was about to say, "If only your mother could have seen you," but he caught himself in time. But he could say it to himself, and mean it with all his heart. "How do you feel?"

Peggy waved the lemon. "Fine, except I wish it was time for the senior stuff."

George French laughed. "It will be, soon enough."

"Well," Balsom suggested, "I guess we'd better go, Peggy. Your turns in the freestyle were very good, but maybe just a little higher with your feet next time. You might need it. And remember what I told you about your start in the backstroke." He put his hand on her shoulder. "Good luck."

Sam leaned down quickly and kissed her wet forehead. "Go to it, honey."

The speaker was calling the contestants for the senior backstroke when Sam and Balsom moved along the aisle to where Billy waited, scarcely able to tear his eyes away from the scene below. "Come on!" he urged. "They're going to start!"

Again Peggy had an outside lane, the far one. To Sam, she seemed a lot smaller than she had when lining up with the intermediates. But these were seniors, some of them three or four years older than she. She slid into the water, did one practice pushoff, then slowly came back and waited, her hand on the edge of the overflow.

"There's Marie Phillips, in the nearest lane," Balsom said.

Sam looked down. The Phillips girl was finishing her warmup and her strokes were easy and relaxed, her speed steady.

"Notice how she takes a little glide between strokes?"

45

Balsom pointed. "That's a rest period, and one that can count."

Sam turned to him. "Does Peggy do that?"

Balsom nodded. "They all do it. It's standard form. Or was, until people started breaking records by straight flailing, with no glide. I was mentioning earlier about Yale. They cut the glide out. But it takes a lot more out of the swimmer, and is awfully hard to sustain, although it sure counts in speed." He looked down suddenly. "They're ready—"

Sam was watching Peggy when the gun cracked. She shot backward as if propelled from a catapult, and she was the first one up and stroking. Her lead was a good two yards. Beside Sam, Balsom was tense, his brows puckered in concentration. Sam could hear him counting under his breath.

As they approached the far end, the others were gaining on Peggy, and Marie Phillips was almost stroke for stroke with her.

"Watch her turn!" Balsom snapped. "Because here's where she wins or loses!"

Neck and neck, on opposite sides of the pool, Peggy and the Phillips girl touched and went into the twisting, churning flip turn, feet flashing high.

"Peggy beat her!" Balsom breathed, fists clenched and pounding the rail. And Sam saw that he was right. The two had gone into the turn as one, but Peggy was smaller and faster, and when they broke surface and were stroking again, she was almost a length in front.

"Hold it, Peggy—hold it!" Balsom muttered as, inch by inch, Marie Phillips moved up on her.

Beside them, Billy was screaming Peggy's name.

Again they approached the end of the pool, and again they were stroke for stroke and Peggy's lead was gone. And

46

then, as they touched, Peggy was like an otter, her turn so fast Sam couldn't follow the motion. And once again, when they broke surface, stroking into the last lap, she was almost a length ahead.

"Hold it, Peggy!" Balsom repeated. "Hold it!"

Slowly, inexorably, Marie Phillips drew up on her until only a foot separated them. They were nearing the end of the pool, and the tempo of their swimming and the smashing waves of noise from the crowd seemed to swell together. Then suddenly it was over, and Sam could not see who had won. The noise ceased abruptly as the public-address system hummed.

"Winner of the senior backstroke—" there was a pause, and it was as if every person in the gallery had stopped breathing—"Porter!"

The roar of the crowd was deafening. Sam was limp. He looked across to the little band of rooters in the Birchwood section. Some of them were screaming. Others simply looked stunned.

"Yea . . . Peggy!" Billy crowed exultantly. "Now what do you think, you mudheads?"

"Billy!" Sam said sternly. But he couldn't blame the boy.

"Bless her heart," Balsom said. "You've got a real swimmer in your family, Mr. Porter. A tremendous one."

Sam could only nod.

"You remember," Balsom said, "that I told you she was great in practice. But it was a matter of finding out what she'd be like in competition. Some people are overwhelmed by it. They freeze. Others revel in it, and can do their best only when the going is roughest. Well, that's the way your daughter is."

Sam looked up at the clock. "How long will she have to rest before the freestyle?"

47

"About half an hour." Balsom eyed him thoughtfully for a moment. "I'm going to slip down for a few minutes. But I think I should go alone, if you don't mind."

"Go ahead," Sam said. He leaned back and watched the crowd. On every side, the talk was of Peggy. He smiled inwardly. She had earned it. After this day's work, she should never be lonely at school again, or left out, or passed by. By tonight she'd be the queen of Birchwood. He turned to Billy. "Some sister you've got, boy!"

Billy's hair was mussed, and his face was wreathed in a grin. "Isn't she, though!" he said, his eyes alight, his young voice fairly sparkling with pride. "I wish it was time for the freestyle."

Sam shook his head. "Peggy's going to need all the rest she can get."

Together they watched the breast-stroke race, waiting for the call that would bring Peggy back out the door from the dressing room. Finally Balsom appeared, pushing his way along the aisle.

"How is she?" Sam asked anxiously.

"She's tired," Balsom said. "But she's pretty excited too. And I think that may help to sustain her."

"I sure hope so."

The loud-speaker came on. "Senior girls' freestyle," the announcer said. This time Peggy was in the center lane, and Marie Phillips was in lane two, right next to her.

At a word from the starter, the girls took their positions. Together they crouched forward arms back. Then came the crack of the pistol. In a single, fluid motion Peggy appeared to fall forward, her arms swung out in front and she gave a tremendous pushoff kick. She hit the water almost flat and broke surface stroking easily. For a second Sam thought she had got away in front, but there was Marie Phillips right beside her, matching her stroke and

48

rhythm. Before they had gone half the length of the pool, it was as if there were only the two of them in the race.

"Here we go," Balsom said, and as the girls approached the end of the pool Sam heard him begin to count. Then they were into the turn, and Balsom's shout burst in Sam's ears as Peggy broke half a length in front. "She can win it on those turns!"

Sam watched the two girls and the roar of the crowd was so great that the whole place took on the quality of a dream; it was almost as if he were alone in a little bubble of silence, and when he spoke he could not hear his own voice. The gallery was alive with noise and movement and he knew they were shouting for his little girl.

Peggy and Marie Phillips were getting closer to the other end of the pool now, and again they were swimming a duet, shoulders and backs scarcely in the water at all, churning feet sending a double wake out behind them.

"Now watch this!" Balsom said hoarsely. "Watch it!"

Sam watched as the girls touched the end of the pool and flashed into almost perfectly matching flip turns, both giving tremendous pushoffs. Sam felt his heart almost stop as Marie Phillips broke water two feet ahead of Peggy.

And then suddenly Peggy was up and stroking and the crowd came to its feet, shouting as if to burst the very walls, and Sam's own voice was lost in the noise and Balsom was pounding his arm. Because gone was Peggy's smooth, relaxed stroke. Instead, she was flailing, her arms churning the water like a pair of windmills, her feet sending out a wake like that from an outboard motor. She was past Marie Phillips and almost a length in front before the older girl realized what had happened.

Abruptly she, too, switched into the power stroke and took up the challenge. And then the homestretch duel was on.

"Swim, Peggy . . . swim, Peggy!" Sam shouted, and when he stopped for breath he was surprised to hear his cry continued. Across the gallery in the Birchwood rooters' section, all the youngsters were on their feet. "Swim, Peggy . . . swim, Peggy . . . swim, Peggy!"

Down in the water it was as if Peggy could hear, and she appeared to be swimming as if her very life depended on it. Beside her, Marie Phillips was inching up with every stroke, her thrusting hands even with Peggy's elbows, her powerful shoulders and long training beginning to take their toll.

"Swim, Peggy . . . swim, Peggy . . . swim, Peggy!" The cry shook the gallery, and then suddenly the race was over, and the noise was deafening. But Sam could not speak. He saw George French jump into the pool with all his clothes on, and then they were lifting Peggy out onto the edge of the pool, and someone was helping Marie Phillips out, and then the two girls were sitting there with their arms around each other, and then Sam could not see them because of the people gathering around. He felt Balsom's hand on his arm.

"She'll be all right," Balsom said. "There's a doctor with her."

At the first hum and crackle of the loud-speaker, the gallery was as silent as a vacuum, and Sam held his breath.

"The winner of the senior girls' freestyle," came the voice of the announcer, "Porter, of Birchwood."

The word "Birchwood" was lost in the roar of the crowd, and Sam had to fight to hold back the tears. Beside him, Billy was jumping up and down screaming, "She won! Peggy won!"

Billy stopped abruptly and stared across the gallery, and Sam followed his gaze. In the Birchwood section the cheerleader was standing in front of his companions, arms pounding out the beat as with one great voice they roared:

"P-o-r-t-e-r . . . *Porter!*"

And as the sound echoed and reverberated up in the arched roof of the new Williams Collegiate pool, Sam heard Balsom's voice, "Let's go, Mr. Porter."

Now, sitting in the living room, with Peggy upstairs doing her homework, Sam was troubled and uneasy. Peggy had started swimming because she was lonely, and felt left out. The purpose had been to win friends, to become one of the crowd, to gain the acceptance every youngster seeks. Now she had that acceptance. But if he had heard right, she planned to refuse it.

He lit a cigarette and turned away from the fireplace to gaze out the window at the street. A light snow was falling and around every street lamp swirled a glowing halo of diamonds. This was their home. This was where Peggy would finish growing up. This town was their future. And if she rejected the offer of friendship, she would destroy every chance she might have to make herself really a part of the town.

He left the living room and went to the foot of the stairs. "Peggy?"

"Yes, Daddy."

"Would you come downstairs a minute?"

He went back into the living room, and she came in behind him, a book in one hand and a pencil stuck into the hair over one ear. "What is it, Daddy?"

Sam took a deep breath. "I heard what you said to Billy in the kitchen."

For a moment she looked at him. Then she gave a faint shrug.

"Peggy, have you ever done something very wrong, and very inconsiderate, and wanted to make amends?"

Peggy frowned uncertainly. "I—I don't know."

Sam looked at her, his eyes steady on hers. "I think it would be terrible to want such a chance and be denied it. Don't you?"

Peggy's frown deepened. "But Daddy, I don't know what you mean!"

"Okay, honey. I guess you'd better get back to your homework." Sam stood a moment, hearing her footsteps on the stairs, and then the click of her bedroom door closing.

And then the front-door chimes pealed. Sam went out into the hall and opened the door. Three girls stood on the porch, their heads in scarves, their arms loaded with books. One of them, in a blue coat, smiled.

"Is Peggy home?"

"Yes, she is. Won't you come in?"

As they entered, the girl in the blue coat said, "We're all going over to Angie's house to have a homework party." She ended on a rising note.

Sam stared. "A what?"

The girls giggled. "We play records and do our homework. We wondered if Peggy would like to come."

Sam closed the door behind them. "Well," he said, "I don't know. I'll call—"

"I'm right here, Daddy."

Sam turned. She was standing halfway up the stairs. He said, "The girls want to know if you'd like to go over to Angie's house for a homework party with them. Would you?"

In the silence of the hall, Sam could hear the gentle rhythmic ticking of the big clock, and the sound of his own breathing. Peggy's gaze met his own. She opened her mouth to speak, then closed it. She looked at the girls and then back to him. And he could see tears brimming in her blue eyes.

She swallowed once, and then she spoke—and it seemed to Sam that she addressed herself more to him than to the girls. "Why, yes," she said. "I'd like to, very much. I'll get my books." Then she turned and scurried up the stairs.

Sam smiled at the girls. "She'd like to, very much," he said. And then he went to the hall closet to get her coat.

Medal for Mums

GERTRUDE CRAMPTON

Mary Jo Wagner straightened her dress so that it hung from her shoulders as the designer had intended. Every time she asked to be taken above the merchandise floors of Lamson's to the executive floor, the elevator operator looked her over quite carefully as though wondering why in the world she was entitled to enter the carefully guarded offices.

"Maybe I ought to explain that I'm Sally Wagner's little girl and my mama writes advertising copy," Mary Jo reflected a bit sourly as she stepped to the rear of the elevator car. If she got just one dose today of the customary, "Sally, don't tell me this is your *daughter!*" she was going to be violently and nauseatingly sick. As though she were some sort of thumb-sucking monstrosity no mother in her right mind would admit owning. As though—Mary Jo shrugged her irritation away. No sense in getting worked up over past events.

Today was going to be a good day. Mums herself had
said so. "Pick me up at the office at twelve," she had suggested. "We'll lunch." Mary Jo wished they'd eat lunch
some place other than Lamson's. Mums was so definitely
the executive type in Lamson's dining room and couldn't
forget it. "Then," Mums had rattled on, "we'll pick out
a new dress for these ever-increasing dates with Tucker,
and afterwards we'll go to the matinee. There's quite a nice
musical at the Imperial, and we might as well take it in.
It's about time we went off on a bat together."

Yes, today was going to be a good day, Mary Jo reflected
as the car shot upward, and she wasn't going to be irritated
by any of the things that always seem to happen when you
have a career-mother instead of a mother-mother. White
gloves gleaming, every hair in place, stocking seams ruler-
straight, Mary Jo swung down the hall of the eighth floor
to her mother's office.

"The thing to do," Mums was saying to one of her
assistants as Mary Jo walked in, "is to shift the sweater ad
and the skirt ad to Thursday—by the way, if Fred doesn't
perk up his artwork a little, we can't interest the teen-agers
—and then we'll . . ." Mums glanced up, looking Mary
Jo over in a puzzled, withdrawn way. Suddenly, with a
flash of recognition: "Oh, Mary Jo! Look, dear, something's come up. I just can't get away. We've got to shift
all our ads for days and days to make room for some stuff.
You know how it is." Mums fumbled in her bag and
brought out two pink tickets. "Telephone TwoGees and
ask her to come in for the matinee. See you later, darling,
and forgive me this once." Before Mary Jo could protest
that TwoGees couldn't possibly get into town by matinee
time, Mums' head was bent again over drawings and advertising copy and schedules.

"Have lunch downstairs while you're waiting for Two-

Gees," Mums called to Mary Jo's retreating back. "Charge it to me."

Mary Jo walked glumly to the elevator. Advertising executive! Now, there was something she definitely was not going to be.

As for eating downstairs, Mary Jo wasn't going to have anything to do with Lamson's or Lamson's restaurant, or Mums' charge account. Instead, she stopped at a drugstore and had a limp sandwich and a malted before she caught the next suburban train home. A swell Saturday, not!

Going home was unthinkable, Mary Jo concluded as she got off the commuters' local at Glen Ridge. She was so miserable she needed company, and if she went home, she'd just wail. Her well-shod feet turned in almost instinctively at TwoGees house. TwoGees, known only to her family in moments of deep stress as Grace Geraldine, could be counted on to lend a sympathetic ear or donate a cheering phrase. Mary Jo tore the pink matinee tickets into defiant bits and rang TwoGees' doorbell. TwoGees' mother answered.

"Hello, Mary Jo. Don't tell me you could smell fudge all the way into town," she challenged smilingly. "Run along to the kitchen. TwoGees and your usual flock are slowly knocking the house down from there."

Golly, there was a mother for you, Mary Jo decided. TwoGees was really important in her mother's life. She didn't have to be sandwiched in between sweaters and skirts and how Fred's artwork happened to be coming along.

The flock, as TwoGees' mother called them, was in the kitchen: TwoGees and Herb, Flossie and Dale, Kit and Mac, and trying hard not to look like an extra, Tuck.

"Hi!" said TwoGees. "Boy, howdy, am I glad to see you! Now Tuck won't be the lost lamb."

Tuck grinned delighted agreement and handed Mary Jo a plate of fudge. "TwoGees' mother broke down and gave us a cup of sugar," he explained. "We got the other cup from Flossie's mama."

"Just a minute, careless." TwoGees had an eye on Mary Jo's white gloves. "Our cultured friend has been to the city. Let her get rid of her city slicker clothes before she tries fussing around with this gooey stuff."

"Been up to monkey business with your ma?" Tuck smiled as he took Mary Jo's hat. "Your mother's slick. I give her the diamond bracelet for being least like a mother of all the mothers in Glen Ridge."

"And you're not fooling," added Mary Jo silently.

"No stuff," Tuck went on, "she's swell. Smart and cute and easy to be around. I guess it's her work that keeps her so sort of young."

"Did I tell you I saw her in Lamson's the other day?" Kit asked. "She looked keen. She said she was running around getting ideas for ads, but she took me in to a friend of hers at the soda bar, and they rigged up something pretty special." Kit wriggled blissfully. "Imagine working in a store with a soda bar."

"Yeah, imagine!" Mary Jo retorted, and got another station on the kitchen radio.

There was a queer silence, and Tuck looked at Mary Jo sharply.

"Let's dance," he said suddenly, and held out his arms. Some of the others were dancing, too, when TwoGees' mother poked her head into the kitchen, smiled approval, and withdrew. Mary Jo sighed heavily.

"Trouble, Mary Jo?" Tuck squeezed her hand lightly, but Mary Jo would not admit any difficulties. After all, she wasn't going to discuss Mums in front of the kids. She smiled at Tuck's concerned face and shook her head.

58

"No trouble, Tucky. Just pure bliss. We should do this more often."

"Now you're talking," agreed Tuck.

"We'd already decided before you got here, Mary Jo," Mac chimed in.

"Once a week on Fridays," said Kit.

"And who do you suppose is first goat?" Flossie waggled a finger.

"Not me?" Mary Jo was dismayed.

"You," Tuck assured her. "Good old you!" He folded Mary Jo's hand in his. "Come on, wench. I'll walk you home. Fudge's all gone."

He led Mary Jo out the back door and down the sidewalk.

"You're not fooling me, Mary Jo Wagner." Tuck was mockingly fierce. "Something's bothering you, and you might as well tell Pappy."

"Pappy, yet?" laughed Mary Jo.

"Sure, Pappy—when you're in trouble. Come on, now, spill it to Papa. Is it having the gang at your house first?"

Mary Jo chewed her lip thoughtfully. "No, it isn't having the gang first, or last. It's having the gang, period."

"Well, my gosh!" Tuck disbelievingly stared at her. "Don't you like the kids?"

"Sure I like the kids," Mary Jo replied indignantly. "But can't you see that things are different at my house?"

Tuck's puzzled look was answer enough.

"Well, golly, Tuck, the other kids' mothers are home all the time."

"So what?" Tuck demanded.

"So when it comes to planning a thing like this, I feel so all alone."

"All alone, my foot," Tuck scoffed. "In the first place,

59

this isn't a banquet Friday, and in the second place, you've got twice the help Flossie and TwoGees have. Your mother'd do anything for you, and you've got Martha besides. Your mother's swell, and so's your housekeeper."

Tuck peered down through the dusk at Mary Jo's troubled face. "My gosh, you're not sore at your mother, are you? I mean, just because she can write ads better than she can wash dishes? There's nothing to get sore at her about. She can't help it. Some women are talented at keeping house, and some do better at other stuff. It isn't their fault. You gotta do what you gotta do.

"What do you care, anyhow? Your mother's a swell person—always looks nice, always knows what to talk about with the gang, and dances better than anybody I ever saw—for her age, I mean. I should think you'd be proud of her." Tuck continued to stare at Mary Jo. "Why, you're not proud of her. You're—Mary Jo!—you're jealous of her. Jealous of your own mother."

"I am *not!*" Mary Jo tore her hand from Tuck's grasp. "I am not! I just think she ought to stay home and settle down. And you don't have to be so fatherly, either. I didn't ask for your advice."

"Don't worry," said Tuck. "You've heard the last of it—if that's the way you feel."

Mary Jo banged into the house, and Mums and Dad left their discussion hanging in mid-air. Law or copywriting, Mary Jo wondered how Mums could be so interested in law cases and Dad in copywriting.

"I'm terribly sorry about today," Mums said, forcing a smile to her tired face. "Did you and TwoGees enjoy the matinee?"

"We didn't go," Mary Jo replied woodenly. "TwoGees couldn't have got into town in time."

"But, honey, you could have left her ticket at the box

office. She wouldn't have missed more than a little of the first act," Mums protested.

"Well, we didn't go," said Mary Jo defiantly. "I didn't want to, anyway."

"What did you do with the tickets?" Dad asked. "Tear 'em up?"

"Yes, I did." Mary Jo was still defiant.

Dad laughed. "Hope you enjoyed that little gesture three dollars and sixty cents' worth. Three-sixty is what you'd have got back at the box office, you know, if you'd turned them in."

Before Mary Jo could reply, Martha announced dinner.

"Good!" Mums was enthusiastic. "I'm starved. Hope you're having something good, Martha."

TwoGees' mother would know exactly what her family was having for dinner, Mary Jo reflected angrily. She'd know because she'd have bought it and cooked it. Mums didn't know from one day's end to the next what was in the house.

Dinner was a silent meal, as far as any contribution from Mary Jo went. Not until Martha brought in angel food for dessert did she stir.

"How about making one of these for the gang, Martha?"

"Sure," Martha replied agreeably. "When?"

"And why?" asked Mums.

"We decided to get together one night a week to sort of brush up on our dancing," Mary Jo explained. "I'm elected for next Friday. I tried to get out of it."

"Sounds like fun," Mums offered.

Dad nodded agreement. "Why try to get out of it?"

"Only not next Friday," Martha stated. "At least not for one of my angel foods."

"Glory, that's right!" Mums exclaimed. "You're taking a long weekend to visit your sister, aren't you?"

"Yes, I leave Wednesday night."

"Oh, oh," groaned Dad. "That's five restaurant dinners I'll have to buy. Martha, Martha, why do you have to have a sister? Or why didn't I marry a good cook?"

Martha giggled, and only Mums knew that the thought behind Mary Jo's resentful frown was, "Yes, why didn't you?"

Martha smiled apologetically at Mary Jo, and Mums reached around the table to pat her hand. "After all, honey, the kids'll live without angel food this once. We'll get something nice from the bakery."

"I *wanted* angel food—homemade angel food!" Mary Jo said stormily and left the table.

Up in her own room she pounded the pillow with her fist.

"What's the matter with me?" she demanded of the shadowed walls. "Martha thinks I'm crabby. Tuck is sure I'm jealous. I've hurt Mums' feelings. And Dad thinks I'm a goon.

"What a day! Tuck's probably right when he says people are what they are. Anyway, why should Mums want to be what I want her to be? I wish she did, though," Mary Jo sighed, with complete lack of logic. "I wouldn't feel so out of it if she did."

The days went by, and though Mary Jo tried to snap out of her blue mood, everything seemed to contrive to make her feel more and more depressed, and more and more irritated with her mother. Monday Flossie wore the new Jacquard sweater her mother had made for her. Tuesday Kit refused to join the gang for Cokes. Her mother had agreed to make her a new date dress, and Kit was going to do the ironing so as to give her mother more time for sewing. Wednesday Dad took Mums and Mary Jo to the church supper, and there was TwoGees' mother cutting pies and passing salad and just about running the whole affair. And for the crowning touches, Tuck didn't come near her, didn't call her up, and Mums didn't mention Friday night.

Mary Jo had never felt so completely alone in her life, or so completely sorry for herself. It wasn't any of Tuck's business how she felt about her mother, but—suppose he just kept on staying away? It was just too much! Somehow, the whole wretched episode seemed to revolve around angel food, and Mary Jo was resolved, suddenly, to have angel food Friday night. On Thursday she skipped lunch to confer with TwoGees' mother.

"Martha's away," Mary Jo finished her explanation. "And you know Mums."

"Indeed I do know your mother," TwoGees' mother replied. "One of the finest, brightest, kindest women in Glen Ridge. And a real credit to the community. You should be proud of her."

"Oh, sure, sure!" It was silly to offend TwoGees' mother. "But you know Mums and cooking. My gosh, I'll bet she doesn't know how to light the oven."

TwoGees' mother still looked severe. "That may be, but your mother is talented along other lines."

Mary Jo nodded. "But not along lines that will get me an angel food cake for the gang."

TwoGees' mother laughed. "I'll bake your cake for you, honey."

"Oh, no!" Mary Jo was very earnest. "I want to bake this myself."

"To show Mother?"

"To show Mother," Mary Jo nodded.

"Very well," TwoGees' mother agreed. "I'll stand on the side lines and coach."

On Friday Tuck unbent enough in Latin class to say

abruptly, "Guess I won't be able to make it tonight, Mary
Jo. Uh—I'm going to be busy."

"Oh," said Mary Jo. She could feel the red creeping up
into the roots of her hair. "Oh, that's all right, Tuck. See
you Monday."

She ducked out of Latin class fast. Let him stay away, if
he felt that way about it. She was going through with her
plans just the same.

And so Friday afternoon, while TwoGees practiced with
the basketball team, Mary Jo shopped and carried eggs and
cake flour and sugar and almond extract to TwoGees'
kitchen and was instructed in the art of baking angel food
cake.

"There's really nothing to it," TwoGees' mother assured
her. "Just a light hand and a good egg beater."

There might be nothing to it, but Mary Jo was proud as
the vainest peacock when she took her cake from the oven
after its hour of slow baking. High, light, delicately
browned, with tantalizing whiffs of almond.

"It's a beauty," TwoGees' mother congratulated her.
And when it was cool, she put it into her covered cake dish
so that Mary Jo could carry it easily.

Mary Jo slipped quietly in the front door and put the cake
dish on the top shelf of the coat closet.

"Just wait till I bring this out for the kids in front of
Mums," she reflected, while another part of her mind
wondered why in the world she was making such an issue
of angel food. "Just wait till she sees this. This'll show
her."

She had just closed the door when Dad came in.

"Hi!" He grinned companionably. "I'm dead. Let's get
your mother and go to some nice place for dinner. You
know, *serviettes* instead of napkins. Mums is probably
upstairs."

They had just started up the stairs when they suddenly heard a clatter from the kitchen.

"Our Mums in the kitchen?" Dad murmured. "It can't be."

The two of them hurried through the swinging door that led to the kitchen. There was Mums, all right, her slick coiffure tumbled every which way, her face well smudged, and tears trembling in the brown eyes that were usually so gay.

"Oh, Mary Jo!" she wailed. "I wanted so much to surprise you. And I thought that even if I can't cook and hate to cook, I could just this once. I got Mrs. O'Lone, that nice food demonstrator at the store, to tell me exactly how to make an angel food cake, and I came home at noon to do it, and I tried so hard. And look at it!"

Mary Jo didn't even glance toward the tubular pan. She couldn't have seen it anyway for the great, blinding wave of love and affection. Lots of mothers baked cakes and knitted sweaters and made dresses for their daughters. But they knew how. That was their job and their career. But Mums, who could turn a neat phrase and hardly knew one end of an egg beater from the other, Mums had worked and fussed and burned her hand and undertaken a job she knew nothing about, just to please her.

"I don't know whether I stirred when I should have folded, or used too much sugar, or jarred the oven, or what. But it's such a mess!" Mums wept.

Mary Jo threw her arms about her mother. "Who cares about the old cake?"

"Now, before both you girls are washed away in your own tears, let's get practical." Dad's voice held a reassuring note. "There isn't a thing the matter with this cake except that it puffed down instead of up. It tastes pretty good. The thing to do is to split it in half. Then nobody'll know it was

65

always kind of stunted. On the way home from dinner we'll buy some ice cream to put in the middle and make ice-cream sandwich cake."

Mums brightened. "We could, couldn't we? And get a big jar of chocolate syrup to put over the whole thing."

Mary Jo was very definite. "Much more dreamy than plain old angel food."

Relieved and happy, Mums hurried upstairs to repair the damage of one afternoon in the kitchen.

"Kind of cute of her at that, wasn't it?" Dad grinned and opened his newspaper. "Where are you going, Mary Jo?" he demanded as out of the corner of his eye he caught the flick of the opening front door.

"Just a little errand," Mary Jo answered, holding Two-Gees' mother's cake dish concealed by the door. "I'll be back before Mums is ready."

"All right," Dad waved affably. "Ask Tuck to go to dinner with us if you like."

Mary Jo wandered down the street, wondering what in the world to do with her beautiful angel food. The Wagners' garbage can certainly would not do, and you can't just toss a cake into the street.

"What are you doing, roaming around with that thing?" demanded a shadowy figure.

"Oh, Tuck! What in the world am I going to do?" Mary Jo was so relieved to see him that she poured out the whole story. "It isn't just that I don't want Mums to know how mean I was going to be, flashing the cake on her in front of the gang. She worked so hard, Tuck, at something she didn't know anything about, just to please me. I can't let her see this cake. And I can't think of any place to throw it."

Tuck lifted the cover. "Throw *this* away?" Real horror was in his voice. "We'll just slide this under my work-

66

bench. There's nothing handier around a workbench on a Saturday afternoon than a nice angel food cake."

Tuck fumbled with the cake box and fumbled, too, for words. "Uh, Mary Jo, look. Mary Jo, I'm not going to be so awfully busy, after all. About tonight. I mean, if it's all right, Mary Jo?"

Mary Jo grinned up at him. "Swell, Tucky. I'm all right, too, now. Are you too busy to go out with Mums and Dad and me for dinner?"

"Heck, no. Just give me time to get rid of the loot and arrange me coils." Tuck galloped toward his house. "Wait for Pappy."

"I will," Mary Jo promised, "I will." She stretched her free arms up to the dim sky. Now that that wretched angel food was gone, she felt a thousand times freer, a million times happier. What a mellow night! What a swell, swell night for the gang! Everything was perfectly perfect again.

"And Martha herself never made a finer angel food cake," Mary Jo reflected, "than the one that Mums made especially for me."

Stop Calling Me Baby

LOIS DUNCAN

THERE ARE eleven maple trees between our house and the Tutters', eleven maple trees and thirty-two cracks in the sidewalk. The summer that I was fifteen, the maple trees were green and full and their shade fell in large, dark patches across the hot sidewalk except in the morning when it fell in the street. I must have walked up and down that sidewalk a thousand times that summer, always slowly, always casually, looking at the maples and cracks in the cement.

"Where are you going?" asked Vandy as I pushed back my chair from the table and started to get up.

"Out," I said shortly.

"Where?"

"For a walk."

Mother said, "Karen, you've hardly touched your dinner. Is anything the matter?"

"No," I said irritably, "nothing's the matter; I just want to go out for a walk. Does anybody have any objections?"

Vandy said, "I'll come with you." She got up too. Vandy was eleven.

"No," I said furiously. "You will not. I'm going by myself."

Vandy's blue eyes filled with tears. She said, "You're horrid. You're always horrid; you never let me do anything any more."

Mother said, "Karen, don't you think—"

I left the room and went out onto the porch and slammed the screen door behind me. It was early evening. The sun still slanted through the trees and fell halfheartedly on the pavement, the way it does on summer evenings when the dark comes slowly and there is a muffled clatter of silverware and a blur of voices from open doors and windows.

The Tutter house, almost at the end of the block, was larger than ours, although Mr. and Mrs. Tutter lived there by themselves most of the time, with the girls married and Joe away at school. I had never been inside, but I was sure I knew how it would be: a hall and then a living room with a grand piano which Mrs. Tutter sometimes played, and beyond that the dining room. Upstairs the main bedroom looked out over the lawn, and Joe's room was on the first floor around to the side.

Joe was in the driveway washing the car.

I concentrated on the trees as I passed him—ten—eleven —twelve—and I went on slowly to the corner and around it. I stood there quietly a moment. Then I turned and started back.

This time, as I passed, he said, "Hi."

I looked up.

"Hi," I said.

He was bent at a stiff, awkward angle, holding a rag in

one hand and the hose in the other, washing the whitewalls. He was wearing an old pair of khaki pants, which covered his legs to the ankles, and a stained white T shirt. I deliberately kept my eyes from his right leg and focused instead on his bristly crew cut and the nose that was bent a little sideways from football.

"Where are you going?" he asked in a friendly way.

"Nowhere special," I said casually. I crossed over and stood beside him, watching him. "When did you get home?" I asked although, of course, I knew.

"About a week ago. I got a ride down from school with some of the fellows."

"Have a good year?" I asked.

"Sure." He looked up at me and grinned. "What's new around here? Let's see, you must be about in the ninth grade by now, right?"

"Tenth," I said, hating him.

"Tenth! Well, gee!" I hated him more than ever.

He straightened slowly and stood back to inspect the tire. He gave it a final slosh with the hose. Then he wrung out the rag and went to turn off the water.

"See you around," he said.

I watched him turn off the faucet and walk up the steps —moving stiffly with one hand on the railing—and go into the house. I heard his voice in the living room, saying something and then laughing, and then his mother's laughter. A few minutes later the light went on in his room. I watched the light for a long time, and when it finally went off I turned and began to walk hurriedly away. I didn't want him to come outside again and find me still standing there.

It was dusk now. The sun was gone and there were no more shadows, but it was hot. Some little girls were playing hopscotch in the street in front of our house.

Vandy broke away from the group and came over to me.

71

"Do you want to play?" she asked. She wasn't mad any more. Vandy never stayed mad.

"No," I said, "I don't."

"You haven't played all summer!"

I started to walk away, and then suddenly I turned back.

"Okay," I said. I tossed in my stone, hopping across the course, turned and hopped back. I picked up my stone and tossed it into the next block. "There," I said, "now I've played. Now leave me alone."

"Okay," Vandy said, "okay. Gosh, you don't have to be so snotty about it."

I went into the house and through the living room and upstairs to my room. Mother and Dad were sitting in the living room, but they didn't say anything as I passed through. I went into my room and closed the door and lay down on the bed. I hadn't eaten much dinner and I was hungry, but I was hungry in another sort of way too. It was a kind of aching feeling, a loneliness that wasn't really loneliness but something else, a feeling of being incomplete. It was a feeling that had started this summer, and it was mixed up in my mind with the heat and the twilight and the maple trees and the children's voices in the street outside.

But it wasn't those things, I thought. Those were a part of every summer I had ever known—they were nothing new. And Joe was nothing new either. He had lived up the block for as long as I could remember. He had washed the car dozens of times and cut the grass and made airplane models in his front yard, and I had hardly noticed. Even that time two years ago when he had been in the automobile wreck —it had been after his senior prom, and I had heard my parents talking about it afterward: "The Tutter boy . . . what a shame . . . to lose a leg at eighteen . . . and I hear he was offered that wonderful football scholarship

. . . such a nice, attractive boy . . . such a terrible pity . . ." I had been sorry, of course, but the pain had not been my pain. I was too busy playing hopscotch with Vandy in the street.

I got up and turned on the light and went over to the dressing table mirror. I looked at myself for a long time. Then slowly I took off my jeans and shirt. I went over to the closet and got the blue taffeta Mother had given me for Christmas and put it on. It was too heavy for summer and a little long; I had never even had it on long enough for Mother to turn it up on me. I went over to my bureau and searched through a top drawer until I found a lipstick.

Vandy came in.

"What are you doing?"

I said, "I thought you were playing hopscotch."

"I was." She came closer. "What are you getting dressed up for?"

"Just because I feel like it. Don't you ever knock before you come into somebody's room?"

Vandy ignored the question. She stood on one foot, as though she were still playing hopscotch.

"They're talking about you downstairs," she said. "Mother and Dad are. Dad says you're acting like a brat this summer and ought to have your bottom whacked even if you are in high school." She smiled importantly. "Mother says to leave you alone. She says you're just going through a stage."

"I'm not!" I said angrily.

"Mother says you are. She says all girls go through it one time or another. *I* won't, though." She looked at me more closely. "Gee," she said, "you look funny in that dress; your stomach sticks out."

I turned to her in cold fury. "Yours does, too," I snapped and added, "and *you've* got a broken front tooth."

Vandy's hand flew to her mouth.

"I don't," she wailed. "It's only a baby tooth." She was dreadfully self-conscious about her chipped tooth.

"It's not," I said coldly. "It's a permanent tooth, and it's broken, and it can never be fixed, and some day it will die and the dentist will have to pull it, and you'll have a big hole there."

"It won't!" screamed Vandy. "It won't!"

She started to cry and ran out of the room. I watched her go with a stab of guilt. No one in our family ever mentions Vandy's tooth.

I turned back to the mirror. The girl who looked back at me couldn't be called pretty, but she did look different—older—with the bright slash of lipstick across her mouth. I sucked in my stomach as tightly as I could, and the dress didn't look bad at all, really.

"Joe," I said softly, experimentally. "Darling." The sound of my voice saying the words frightened me a little. It was so clear-cut and definite when it was put into words that way. I let myself picture his face, the funny bristly hair and the clear blue eyes, and my throat tightened. "Joe," I whispered again, "I know how hurt you must be—how lonely—how empty life must seem for you, after being a big football hero and everything. You can talk to me—I'll understand—I'll try to—to comfort you—"

There was a rap on the door.

"Karen?" Mother's voice was brisk. "I want to talk to you."

I didn't answer, and she opened the door anyway and came in. She looked angry. Then she looked at me and saw the dress and the lipstick, and for some reason her eyes softened.

"What do you want to talk about?" I asked coldly.

"You know very well what," said Mother, sitting down on the end of the bed. "Vandy's in her room crying her heart out because you teased her about her tooth. You know how hard Daddy and I have worked to get her to stop worrying about it."

"Well, that's tough," I said. "Real tough for Vandy. You act as if she's lost a leg or something. If the only thing she ever has to worry about is her tooth, she'll have an easy life."

Mother stared at me as though she hadn't heard me correctly. Then she said, "Baby, what's the matter with you this summer? I don't think I've ever heard you say a thing like that before."

"Nothing's the matter with me," I said rudely, "and please stop calling me 'baby.' "

Mother said, "Karen—" and suddenly, unreasonably, my eyes flooded with tears.

"Leave me alone," I said. "Why can't everybody just leave me alone?"

I pushed hurriedly past her and ran downstairs, through the living room, and out onto the sidewalk again.

It was night now, but not really dark because of the lights from the houses and the street lights, and the eleven maple trees were huge dark masses against the night. I walked quickly now, not bothering to count them. This time I knew I wasn't going to walk casually past the Tutter house. There was an ache inside me, almost too great to bear, and I knew I had to see Joe. It didn't matter if he thought I was completely crazy. I had to see him or I'd die.

I didn't stop to let myself think about what I was doing. When I reached the house, I walked quickly up the porch steps and knocked loudly on the door.

Mrs. Tutter answered it. She came from the living room,

calling something laughingly back over her shoulder. She looked out uncertainly through the screen, not recognizing me on the dark porch.

"Yes?"

"I'm Karen Jackson," I said. "From down the street."

"Oh! Well, come in, dear," Mrs. Tutter said pleasantly, "Is it Girl Scout cookie time already?"

I felt my face flush bright red.

"No," I said, "I just—just—" I had an inspiration. "Mother is baking and she's run out of eggs. She asked me to ask you if she could borrow a couple."

"Why, yes, of course," Mrs. Tutter said graciously. "Come in, Karen, and I'll get them for you."

I followed her through the hall into the living room. It was just the way I had imagined it, spacious and pleasant, with a huge piano in the corner. Mr. Tutter was watching television and there, sprawled on the sofa, was Joe.

"It's the little Jackson girl," Mrs. Tutter said as though she were introducing me for the first time. "Her mother's baking and needs some eggs."

Joe looked up and smiled. "Hi," he said. "I'd hardly have recognized you out of jeans."

"Hi, Joe," I said.

Mr. Tutter nodded at me and tuned down the television. "Some of these summer replacements," he said, "are better than the regular programs."

"Yes," I said, "I guess they are."

Joe hauled himself up and motioned for me to sit down at the end of the sofa. The cushion was warm where his good leg had been. He said, "What are you all dressed up for, Karen? Got a heavy date?"

"No," I said. And then I added carefully, "Not tonight."

"Well, you look awfully nice anyway."

"Thank you." I felt happiness rushing through me in a

76

burning wave. It was almost too much to believe that a moment ago I had been moping in my bedroom and now here I sat, in Joe's home, right on the sofa beside him.

I made myself look at him, straight at him. His eyes were as blue as ever, and his crooked nose made him look oddly vulnerable. I longed to take the rough brown head and draw it down to my shoulder and say aloud the words I had practiced in my room. . . .

Some day, I thought. Next summer, perhaps, or the summer after. He is looking at me now and smiling; it is the beginning.

Mrs. Tutter came bustling back into the room. She had a dish in her hand.

"Are two eggs enough, dear? Are you sure that's all your mother wanted?"

"Yes," I said. "Two eggs."

Joe glanced toward the window.

"It's pretty dark outside. Maybe I'd better walk you home."

I thought for an instant my heart was going to stop beating.

"You don't have to do that. It must be hard for you—I mean, to walk any more than you have to—"

"It'll do him good," Mr. Tutter commented gruffly, his eyes still plastered to the television screen. "He's so restless he's about to tear the house down this summer. Wish Marcy had come with him as we asked her to."

"She couldn't," Joe said. "You know that. Her mother wanted her to go shopping in New York."

"Don't see why she can't get her trousseau here as well as in New York," Mr. Tutter muttered, but there was a note of teasing in his voice. "The way women carry on, you'd think the poor girl was getting something special,

77

instead of a gimpy, flat-nosed college student with two years to go for his B.A. She must be crazy!"

"She is," Joe said, "about me. Lucky girl didn't even have to run very hard to catch me—I couldn't get away from her."

He grinned and his father chuckled and shook his head. It was evidently a familiar exchange. I stared at them both in bewilderment.

"Marcy?" I said. "Who's Marcy?"

"Joe's fiancee," Mrs. Tutter explained. "No matter what those two jokers say, they don't mean a word of it. Pop's just as crazy about her as Joe is."

"Fiancee?" I repeated the word numbly. "You—you're getting married?"

"This fall." Joe swung his legs off the sofa and got a grip on the arm. He held out one hand. "Want to give me a haul up, Karen?"

I shook my head. "No."

"No?" He looked surprised. "Why—"

"You don't need to walk me home." My voice was ragged and strange to my ears, somebody else's voice. "I like to walk by myself. I like to walk in the dark."

An instant later I was in the hall, groping blindly for the door.

"Karen!" Mrs. Tutter's voice flowed after me. "Your eggs!"

The world seemed to be spinning before me. For a moment I clung to the doorknob; then with a tremendous effort I turned and went back into the living room and took the dish with eggs.

I said, "Thank you."

At home I undressed quickly and got into bed. The sheets were cool. I didn't even bother to turn off the lights;

I just lay there feeling the dull ache, the funny, throbbing emptiness. Outside a faint breeze stirred the maples and they rustled, a whispering of leaves moving a little in the summer night, and I thought, "There are eleven maple trees between our house and the Tutters'." Which was a silly thing to think because it didn't matter how far away Joe was, eleven maples or eleven million miles.

I was still lying there with the light on when Mother stopped by the room on her way to bed.

She hesitated in the doorway.

"Karen," she asked, "are you awake?"

"Yes," I said.

Mother said, "I thought you might have gone to sleep with the light on." She came over to kiss me good night the way she always did, just as if I were a baby or something. But this time was different. This time I did not mind.

"Mother," I said, "Joe Tutter's engaged. He's getting married."

"Oh, baby," Mother said softly. "I'm so sorry." The way she said it, I knew she understood, that she had understood all along. Suddenly I was crying: deep, choking sobs, the way I had not cried for years.

"I love him!" I cried. "Mother, I love him so much!"

"I know," Mother said. She did not put her arms around me, she merely sat there and let me cry. "It's hard," she said, "the first summer you love somebody. I remember— it's hard."

"It's not the loving that's hard," I cried angrily. "It's the other part! It's wanting him to love me, too!"

Mother was silent a moment. When she spoke again, her voice was very gentle.

"That will come," she said. "In time. They don't always come together, you know—loving and being loved. If they did, there would be no chance for us to grow."

79

I leaned back against the pillows. Outside the maples moved again, and the breeze slipping through the window was surprisingly cool, almost an autumn-flavored breeze. I drew a long, shaky breath.

"It has been a horrible summer."

"It has," agreed Mother, "for us all. And the worst of it is, we still have it to live through with Vandy."

She smiled and suddenly, to my amazement, I found myself smiling back. We sat there for a long time after that, not mother and daughter the way we had been, but two old friends who had found each other again after a long time apart.

The Reluctant Lilac

CLAE WALTHAM

WHAT HAND swats at life and knocks it awry? Who molds a body? How'd I get here, anyway?

I hold up thick strands of pale hair, arrange them differently on top of my head. It's jute, hemp or sisal; anything but hair. My face is too tan to belong under that sunned-out straw. And my eyes stare from my skinny face like pieces of broken willowware, come upon unexpectedly. All in all, I decide, standing before my mirror, I look like the Churchport town dump after a light, cosmetic snow.

There are times when nothing fits, nothing at all.

I couldn't get back to sleep after the fire engine screamed past this morning. I put on my heavy wrapper and sat in the window, searching the sky for a glow. It must have been a false alarm; the only light was in the east. The sun rises behind Churchport hill. My bedroom looks out toward the bay, which detaches itself from night slowly; layer upon layer of light floats down to lift the bay into day.

And I thought about my parents. I now had problem parents, just like my friends'. Up to yesterday they'd been different. In fact, all the gang think that for family I've the most. My friends squeal to one another about my father's shibui cufflinks. They swoon over the sweaters he wears Saturdays for around-the-housing. Most of all they like the way his hair is graying, just on his temples, better than Hollywood could dye it. Oh, my friends really bleat over this man they call Dreamboat and I call Daddy. As for my mother—well, she still gets whistled at. And holds the permanent cup for the women's sailing event (five years in a row; no one else has done that) .

I used to get along with my parents. People remarked about it. And then if my parents explained I'm their adopted daughter, some of them would say, "*Why, how marvelous!*" or, even more foolishly, they'd say, "*Nobody would know it.*" Some grownups make a specialty of acting foolish. Then last night my parents set off a bomb in the pit of my stomach. Just as I was ready to cut my birthday cake, they informed me that I'm being sent to Brooke School for my junior and senior years.

Did they think this was some kind of present? They said they'd rattle around this old house without me, wouldn't know what to do with themselves and all that jazz. Finally they said they'd brought themselves to this difficult decision reluctantly, for my own good.

For my own good! I'd have bawled right in their faces, but the telephone happened to ring. It was Bob Malone, a piece of the big wood at Churchport High. He's a senior, I'm a sophomore. But a couple of weeks ago, I filed him in the deepfreeze; don't ask me why. When he said he'd pick me up at eight for the movies, I asked if certain people weren't taking certain things for granted. It just popped out; I was talking opposites. And now he asked if he could drop around after breakfast tomorrow, to talk something over with me. In spite of what my parents had just been telling me, I was up there. I mean, I was soaring. I thought about Bob all evening. I promised myself never again to let my tongue slip into reverse and say what I didn't mean. When I finally went to sleep, pictures of Bob Malone were plastered like wallpaper to my dreams. Then the fire engine screamed in this day where nothing fit any more. Lunch was over, and Bob hadn't even telephoned, much less appeared. It's Saturday, so the three of us had sat down to lunch together. My mother gaily said that spring had arrived: she could smell lilacs getting ready to bloom.

For the first time in my life I hated my mother. I looked at her and couldn't figure out why. But that only made the rush of my resentment stronger. No one can smell lilacs getting ready to bloom. My mother's light laughter grated on my nerves like new chalk on old slate. My father said that he, too, could smell lilacs getting ready and opened the French doors onto the terrace. He said the radio had announced some kind of broken weather bureau record. They left their sandwiches and walked onto the terrace together. They spend heaps of time out there, working or reading, or just being parents doing nothing.

My *parents*. I watched their backs from my place at the empty table. And I thought about my second day of being sixteen, and how turning sixteen is having a big ax chop your life in two.

A time comes, maybe not until you're pretty old, say fifteen or sixteen, but a time comes sooner or later—you can't avoid it—when you look in your mirror and ask yourself, *Who am I?*

If you're adopted, there is no answer. All you know is

that you were excess baggage to somebody or other on the day you were born. Later you become classified chattel, and then one fine day, maybe, some IBM machine or other kind of contraption decided who your parents would be.

There they are with their backs to me, the ones the machine decided would be my parents, the ones who lighted the fuse last night. Today, he says the evergreens wintered well, she says the honeysuckle will climb to the lattice top this year.

And they think they're shipping me off to Brooke next September. Well, at sixteen a girl can get a social security number, and with a social security number a girl can get a job. Okay. I guess I know when I'm not wanted. They needn't think I can't take care of myself.

Again I almost bawled, there at lunch, over the sandwiches. And if again the telephone hadn't rung, I would have. It turned out to be Althea Childe, an old friend of my mother's who used to live in Churchport. Her plane to Paris would be delayed at least four hours; she had an unexpected stopover on her way to join her husband, in Europe on business.

We're thirty minutes from Idlewild by taxi. That means my father makes it in twenty-three, like the pilots. The gravel on the drive hadn't resettled itself before my mother started dragging summer chairs to the terrace because, she said, the sun was making a tropics there. Anyway, she went on to explain although I hadn't asked for an explanation, she knew Althea would remember the bay as it used to look from the terrace, before she'd married Henry Childe and moved out west to Minneapolis.

She walked out of earshot and left me standing by the kitchen sink. Her next trip through, I wanted to ask if I should walk down to the store and get something extra for dinner, but she was still talking; I didn't get a word in.

84

". . . Just a lick and a promise, Letitia. Althea's practically family—we don't have to fuss."

I finished the kitchen, straightened up the magazines in the living room, dusted off the bare spaces on our tables and even got a sponge and washed the leaves of the fiddle-leaf rubber plant my mother grows in a big brass pot. I mean, I did everything there is to do in that living room.

Then I went to the terrace to help with the outdoor furniture. My mother talked about Althea Childe, and how old friends are better Investments than A.T.&T. "Gracious! They'll be here any minute. But we're almost ready, aren't we?"

And I managed to get my first word in. "Is there something special you want from the store?"

And my mother said, "I hope Althea doesn't think I've changed much. But it's years since—"

I asked my question a second time. She paid no more attention than if I'd been a crack in the sidewalk. "Mother!" I said.

She turned then. She looked right at me. She said, "Go wash your face and fix your hair. Hurry, Letitia!"

That did it. Okay, okay, if that was the way she wanted it. So I went to my room. It really was warm enough to set some kind of record. I raised my window and looked through the gate in the arbor, down the slope, over the rhododendrons above McCardle's house. Out beyond lay the bay.

And below me the reunion of old friends took place, their laughter spilling on the terrace as they recalled old times. Their voices had a peculiar, remote ring; visitors from another generation. Through their lingo ran the raw excitement of friendship being renewed. It wasn't conversation they made, it was dialogue; they acted parts.

85

"Remember the time we planned to run away, get jobs at Macy's and live in Greenwich Village?"

"Whose mother were we mad at that time?"

My father smiled at them, patiently, like a store Santa Claus. He had on his olive drab sweater and thick-soled sneakers. My mother was in her tweed skirt of lavender and white, and she wore the lavender sweater that gives her what Dreamboat calls iris eyes. Mrs. Childe was turned out for travel and displayed shoes built (so she said) to walk the cobbled streets of Europe from dawn to dark.

I stopped listening. Off there the bay lies, unmoored, a steel platter drifting through space. Every now and then my mother squirms around, and I know what she's thinking. She's thinking that for me not to come down is rude and ungracious. Mother sets great store by sportsmanship and manners.

I set store by nothing.

Why should I? Nothing fits any more. The cracks in my world yawn so wide surely one will swallow me up. And I will be so gladly gone. Silently, with care not to be heard, I raise my window the few more inches it will go.

Mrs. Childe is turning to my father. "You're as handsome as ever, Charley Strawn," she says. "Maybe even handsomer, now your hair's turning so beautifully."

My mother says he's still breaking hearts, says my friends call him Dreamboat. The things mothers tell.

My father rises and bows elaborately. "For that I will open the last bottle of sherry my dad put down. I've been waiting for an occasion grand enough."

Now my mother and her oldest and most cherished friend sit alone. Their voices have the soft steadiness of bees at work. They bring each other up to date on vital statistics.

Silently I lean out. From the softening winter soil a steamy smell of spring rises. My first whiff. I feel it as a visceral thing, this moving into a new season. I think of Bob Malone and I go soft, like a caramel forgotten in the sun.

Through the French doors my father comes. He has a tray with sherry as golden as a wedding ring. There is a mound of beaten biscuits on a plate, and four beautiful glasses that were blown in his great-grandfather's glass factory.

"Expecting someone, Charley?" my mother asks. "I see you have four glasses."

"Letish," my father says, leaving the "ia" off my name as he sometimes does.

"Letitia!" my mother exclaims.

"Well, she's sixteen. And Althea doesn't drop in every day."

There is a flurry of talk about my being sixteen so soon. As if it hadn't taken sixteen long, grim, hard years to get there. I look down on my mother's smoothly brushed dark hair. Spreading out from the crown like spokes are long slivers of white. My mother is quite a tall woman; this was the first time I'd seen her hair from above. Inside me something twists. For the first time in my life I want to stop clocks, tear up calendars, hold back the world and make it stand still in space.

But I am nothing. I am as empty and drifty as the bay. I haven't even a name of my own, except through the courtesy of Charles Strawn and some legal folderol.

Mrs. Childe is chatting gaily. "My girls declare war on me as soon as they get to second grade. I think they teach mother rejection at junior high. How do you and Letitia get along, Anita?"

As if in answer to the question I've been asking myself for a long time, I am aware of my mother saying, "With adopted children, it's different."

I snap my head back into the room. My heart turns back on itself. So she's admitted that it's different with an adopted child. They wouldn't know what to do with themselves rattling around this big old house? Ha! I must prepare for college in the best available school? Double ha! I am being got out from underfoot: their attempt to graft my life onto the Strawn family tree has failed.

I thrust my head out the window, anxious now to hear my mother's every confidence to her old friend. I am careful. I am careful not to make any noise; I know eavesdropping isn't a pretty pastime. But if all's fair in love and war, why not when you're battling to be somebody in your own right? I hold onto the window sill that's been buried under snow and baked under high suns for a hundred years. I need that window sill.

I come in right in the middle of a sentence. My mother has turned to face Mrs. Childe and her voice is up a notch. "—get along too well with Letitia. She doesn't reproach us with our own shortcomings, there isn't enough irritation in our relationship to make her slough us off and establish her own personality. Next year—"

"Anita's right," my father interrupts. "With adopted children parents can't feel guilty for their faults, or conceited for their virtues. It's all too easy just to have fun and spoil them." My father runs his hand through his hair in a quick, short gesture. He is irritated. Whenever something ruffles his feelings, he ruffles his hair.

"Fun! Spoil them! I think you two are just marvelously unselfish the way you've reared Letitia as if she were your very own."

88

"Whose is she, if not our own?" my father asks. Now the irritation shows in his voice and it is brusque.

"Be glad if your children show mother rejection, Allie," my mother says quickly. "They'll get over that, just as you and I did. Charley and I feel we must cut *down* our influence with Letitia, get her to be more independent. So next year we've decided to send her away to finish school, to Brooke—"

"Brooke!" Mrs. Childe says, all exclaimy. "You must be doing very well for yourself, Charley."

"We'll simply continue to be a one-car family for a few more years, that's all." The conversation that was dialogue has turned to talk, rough talk, words flung with white caps.

"Well she's a very lucky girl to have got parents like you," Mrs. Childe says.

My mother twists around in her chair. "We're trying to explain to you, Althea! The idea people have about adoption is crazy, upside down. Why don't people understand?"

"Of course I understand." Now Mrs. Childe's voice has risen. (Old A.T.&.T. has skipped a dividend down there.) "Just the other day I saw in an almanac that over ten per cent of the children in this country are adopted."

"Almanacs and statistics!" My mother's shoulders are stiff and square. "What can they tell you about the feelings of a child?"

My father runs his two hands through his hair and leans forward in his chair. "Adopted kids learn to live with the biggest question mark there is, Althea. It's high time they got a little credit for it."

"Charley! How would Althea know if we didn't tell her?"

My father rises and serves another round of sherry.

"Adopted kids have a subtle bereavement, the loss of something they've never had. Sorry if I blew a stack, Althea. Guess I haven't really thought about adoption since Letish was in kindergarten."

"I understand," says Mrs. Childe quietly, sipping her sherry daintily, smiling.

My parents nod. The squall is over. The visitors from another generation head for the shelter of pleasantries. Shoulders relax, smiles are turned back on.

I clutch the window sill. I'd never been in on a grownup scrap before, much less been the cause of it. I make myself unclench my hands; foolishly, I try to smooth out the indentations my nails have dug. I look out over the bay. I think I see the yacht club launch rounding the point. I think I can make out white moorings piled high in the cockpit. It's hard to know for sure what you see through tears. But I know in a few weeks the first boats will be coming in. I stand and fiddle. I think about what I've heard. It comes to me that maybe my parents had really forgotten I was adopted. Only in my own eyes was I adopted! To them I was simply theirs. *Theirs*. Yes, yes.

I find myself looking into Mother's eyes. Slowly she raises her hand, removes a flake of white paint from her hair.

Something passes between us. Does she move her lips? Do I smile? It doesn't matter. Off there beyond the bay, beyond words and gestures, something takes place between us. Woman to woman, something happens.

She lets the flake of paint drop from her fingers to the terrace. Slowly I turn back into my room. I stand close to the wall and press it hard with open palms. Sometimes things have to get distorted before you can bring them into focus.

I pull away from the wall. I know something now: you know who you are when you can hold up your head even when you're crying. I go to the mirror. You have identity when you look in the glass and say *I'm me!* and it sounds good. Personality is the gift God lets you custom-tailor to fit your individual needs and hopes. I see it now.

I hear the gate in the lattice and Bob Malone's voice. "Oh, I beg your pardon! I heard voices—I thought Tish—" From below comes the sound of polite introductions and light laughter.

"Tish must be asleep," Daddy says. "We may have to get the siren to wake her up."

"Did you hear the fire engine this morning?" Bob asks. "They rushed the inhalator out: my grandfather had another heart attack."

Sounds of sympathetic concern as I quickly flip my hair into its old pony tail. Fashion can wait, Letitia Strawn can't.

"That's why I didn't get over this morning. But I wanted Tish to be the first to know that I got accepted by Boston U. yesterday."

I stare at myself in the mirror. How far is Brooke from Boston? My eyes are a little red, but I don't look too bad. I turn back from the doorway of my room. I want one last look down on the terrace. They sit below like chessmen, each on his own square, separate yet joined. And there's a place waiting for me. I stand another minute feeling beneath my palms the warm, dry, old sill. Next door, along the McCardles' brick wall that catches and holds the sun, I see a glint of lavender. A breeze has sprung up; on it I can smell lilacs.

What fingers open the buds of spring? What hands weave broken patterns into a seamless fabric? Or are there times when everything just fits . . . ?

Girl, you know it.

The Autumn Heart

J. P. FOLINSBEE

THE DOOR of the bus wheezed closed, and Lynn ran from the corner through a misty fall of December rain that was already turning to snow against the darkening sky. It had been such a strange, restless day, almost like spring, yet with an uneasy promise of winter edging the wind.

At the low white gate she paused, waiting until she could walk in, calm and unhurried. The windows of the cottage glinted with light. Her parents would be sitting by the fireplace, then, having coffee. Which was good. Her father loved the open fire on a stormy day. In that, at least, he didn't feel resentfully different and apart.

She brushed a stray lock from her forehead and walked slowly up the path. The storm seemed to have lowered over the house, touching it with foreboding. It was silly to feel that way about your own house, but the bubbling confidence she had felt an hour ago was dwindling away. How could she have been so impulsive—inviting them like that?

"Let's make it definite then," she had called to the gang as the bus had growled away from the curb. *"Friday night at my house."*

She should never have allowed her enthusiasm to flame so high. Bitter experience had taught her to clear such ideas at home before committing herself. Not that her parents would forbid it, but having the gang come to the house, to which they had never before been invited, might be an irretrievable mistake. If her father picked Friday for one of his bad days—which he well might, having visitors thrust upon him that way—she would never again feel the same ease with the gang. They would be embarrassed and sorry, and no matter how understanding they'd try to be, it would spoil things. Still, you couldn't go forever to their houses and never invite them to yours. That, too, would spoil things in time.

She pressed her thumb down crisply on the cold iron latch. Oh, please, she begged silently, let this be one of his *good* days. If only she could get him interested, if she could persuade him to *want* the gang to come.

For a moment they didn't see her. Their gaze seemed lost in the flames of the fire. Standing in the doorway, she almost felt like a little girl again, when they had lived in the tiny, cheerful apartment on Dunbar Street, long before the war and a sniper's bullet had changed their lives. Then, she used to creep out to the living room at night in her sleepers and discover them sitting just like this. Only in those days her father would rise and bound across the room to sweep her up in his arms. He had played football in college, and he had tossed her about like a feather pillow. Now, her mother was sitting alone on the fire bench, and her father was hunched hugely beside her in the aluminum wheel chair he referred to sometimes as his horse and sometimes as his prison, depending upon the day.

"Can just anyone come in?" she asked lightly, and it sounded just right. Casual, with a note of gaiety and spoofing.

They looked up and her heart skipped. He was smiling and relaxed. Almost forty now, he was still remarkably handsome when he smiled, with the distinguished flush of silver in his hair and his black, intense eyes. And her mother had a loveliness, here in the firelight, that washed over the tiredness in her face and made it glow. They were beautiful together. Anyone seeing them would exclaim, "What a happy couple! What a remarkably happy and adjusted family the Jordans are, considering the war left him crippled." But then, a casual observer wouldn't see the other side of this bright, firelit coin.

"So our daughter is home—she has at last learned to come in out of the rain." Her father grinned. "Mother," he gestured extravagantly, "behold your daughter in all the young glory of her seventeen summers." He was joking, in the odd way she knew so well. She let her shoulders relax.

"Behold, indeed," she countered, matching his tone. "Not alone thy daughter, but the newly elected president of the Play Society. Crowned but an hour ago in a strictly fixed election." She stepped grandly down the low ramp into the room and collapsed on the fire bench beside her mother, holding her hands out to the flames.

It was a good start—but how should she go on? Moments like these, with the three of them joking and close to one another, were too precious to be shattered by introducing outside elements and problems. And yet, would there ever be a better time?

"Lynn, how wonderful!" Her mother set her coffee aside,

and rescued her in the casual way they had learned to help each other over awkward pauses. "Now suppose you tell us what it's all about?"

"Well, it's pretty involved," she proceeded carefully. "It's a group at school, you see. A very *select* group, with evening activities and so forth. Mostly the gang."

"Sounds fascinating," her father said wryly. "What gang? And what sort of evening activities, may I ask? Hay rides, sleigh rides—what?"

"Oh, Dad." She laughed. "It's an intellectual group. Strictly on a lofty level. In fact, it's something absolutely new, but Miss Howards, the drama teacher, thinks it's a wonderful idea. And they elected me president for some crazy reason." She wrinkled her nose at him. "I suspect because I'm the only one whose father is a literary man. They're impressed, naturally."

"Oh?" His tone slid warningly offkey. "And just what has all this new-found loftiness to do with me?"

"Oh, nothing, really." *She shouldn't have added that about his being a literary man. Now, already, he was on the defensive.* "I mean, except for the evening activities, perhaps—if you like the idea."

He frowned. "Make sense, Linda Jane," he said, betraying annoyance in the full use of her name. "What exactly are you driving at?"

Her throat went dry. It was useless to act carefree, to try to make things casual and easy and normal. She knew perfectly well that any impending event had to be examined, coldly and ruthlessly, if it affected him. It might prove hurtful and embarrassing, and he was always on guard.

"Well," she kept on, "we plan to meet one evening a week to read and discuss plays. Both old and new plays. Like this week, Miss Howards is picking an old one that none of us has read. Then next week we'll take a modern one. For contrast, you see. And I guess the gang hoped—well, you being a writer and all, that maybe you could help. I mean, with suggestions and things," she ended lamely.

"Why I think it sounds like a marvelous idea," her mother cued in cheerfully. "Doesn't it sound like a fine idea, John?"

Always put things in a positive way. That was one of the rules the doctor at the Veterans Hospital had stressed. "*Paraplegics are very special people,*" he had explained in the lectures they had attended. "*They slip easily into depression. Being immobilized from the waist down makes a man feel helpless. . . .*"

She had been only twelve then, and it had sounded exciting and challenging. She had wanted so desperately to help him. She had been so proud of him. But now, after nearly five years of unpredictable moods and sudden strains, of living in this neat, functional prison of a house, something had happened inside her. She was ashamed of it, but she had begun to hate the chair that she had once regarded as a personal challenge to all of them.

The thought made her look up at him guiltily. It wasn't that she didn't love him still. She did, terribly. But the wheel chair was like a wall, imprisoning them, shutting out the world. It had been all right in the beginning. Then she hadn't minded never having her friends in. But now she was growing up, making new friends, both boys and girls. Her life was widening, not closing in. And she couldn't live totally in an outside world of school and friends. Home had to be a part of it, too. Maybe it was selfish and unworthy, but she had begun to dread coming home after school. It was like walking out of bright sun into deep, strange shadows. . . .

"Doesn't it sound wonderful, John?" her mother re-

97

peated as though she had not said it a first time. That was
another rule. Be patient and pretend. *Pretend, really, until
you were no longer yourself at all.*

He shifted uneasily. "It may be wonderful, but I'd prefer to be left out of it," he said abruptly. His knuckles
began to show white against the cup he held in his hand.
"Why do you persist in keeping up this hoax that I am a
writer? It must be a great joke by now."

"But you are!" Lynn protested. "You're the only person
in Brookside who has ever published stories. And your
play is practically ready, Dad. Everyone—well, everyone
thinks it's wonderful."

"My play is ready to be torn up," he said impatiently.
"I've asked you again and again not to talk about it. Sure,
everyone thinks it's wonderful. They think it's wonderful
that a paraplegic can get out of bed by himself. It's just
plain wonderful!" His face flushed angrily, and suddenly
the cup crashed out of his hand and shattered on the
hearth.

"I'm sorry." Lynn turned and began to pick up the sharp
fragments. She should never have hoped that he would
understand, that he would realize how important it was to
her. Cooped up here, he didn't know what it meant not
to be free to bring kids home, spontaneously, on the spur
of the moment. He didn't know what it meant to live in
two worlds, each locked away from the other. She should
never have asked the gang to come. It was hard enough
for her to understand his moods, and absorb his sudden
explosive angers. She couldn't ask strangers to share that
understanding.

Five years ago, when he had first come home and this
special little house was being built, he had been able to
joke about the trapeze over his bed and his gymnasium
room and the ramps in the doorways. She had been so

sure then, that his fear of meeting new people, his sudden withdrawals into a bitter world of his own, would pass. He would become a famous writer. Their home would become a sort of brilliant Grand Central Station, with wise and interesting people coming to call.

She rose with the broken cup in her hand. What silly fantasies they had been! He didn't want to meet the world, on any terms. Maybe her mother and she had failed him. But *how?* They had encouraged him in his writing, yet after the first half-dozen stories written in a flush of determination, he had begun to tear everything up. And it was the same with everything. . . .

"I'd better put dinner on—it's getting late." Her mother rose. "How would anyone like to eat right here in front of the fire? I can set up a card table in a jiffy."

Lynn glanced up gratefully. "It sounds nice, Mom," she responded. "Dad?"

"Sounds good." He nodded.

"Tell me more about this Play Society, Lynn," he said when her mother was gone. "I didn't mean to lose my temper. I really am interested."

He was trying. They all kept trying. But it was meaningless, because it kept revolving back to the closed circle of the three of them. Even if they smoothed it over, she would never feel right about having the gang Friday. It would be better to just resign from the group. Somehow she could make excuses that would satisfy both them and him. Certainly, if she wanted to keep up at all, she couldn't have them because her father might flare up—or worse, sink into a depression that would hang like a pall over the evening. It would be far better to just break away and stick to activities that were confined to school.

"It's nothing much, really." She mustered a smile. "Just a crazy notion some of us had. We thought it could be fun and a little different. But you know how such things go, it probably won't amount to anything." She bent down and put her arms around his shoulders. "I'm sorry I was stupid about it and disturbed you with a lot of girlish prattle."

"I suppose, your being president," he said softly, "you would naturally want to hold the first meeting here. The others would expect it."

"No. As a matter of fact . . . ." She hesitated and moved away. "As a matter of fact, we haven't even planned that far, you see, it's all sort of in the beginning stages." Why couldn't she think of something clever and believable? Anything. She turned, and he was watching her, obviously seeing through the thin fabric of her evasion. His gaze held steady for a moment, then his eyes dropped to his lap.

"Your mother and I could go out to a show," he said carefully. "Then—well, there wouldn't be anyone to interfere."

She had hurt him. In trying to protect him from the truth, she had hurt him as deeply as though she had hurled her disappointment at him in a towering rage. It was impossible—like one of those ridiculous rocking toys that no matter how you set them down always bobbed mockingly to their feet. She stared at him rebelliously. Didn't it matter that he had hurt her, too? That for years she had given in to *his* whims, *his* wishes? And just this once, when it mattered so much to her, he might have been gracious, instead of turning her hopes into feelings of guilt.

If only she could put it into words. If only she could turn on him and say, *"I'm not ashamed to have my friends meet you. Why do you always make me feel as though I thought you were a skeleton in the family closet, to be*

shunted off to the movies every time company comes?"
But, of course, she couldn't say it.

"We'll arrange something," she said at last. "Please
don't worry about it, Dad. It isn't important."

"Except to you," he replied quietly. She looked at him,
startled. His shoulders seemed hunched in defeat as he
stared into the fire.

A burning flush rose to Lynn's face and she glanced
guiltily down at her hands. They were doubled into fists.
So he had sensed and seen the anger she thought she was
hiding so well! She forced her fingers to go limp, and sat
down quietly on the fire bench beside him.

"Oh, Dad." She took his hand. It was still powerful. An
athlete's hand. "I am sorry."

"I think you'd better ask your play people to come on
Friday," he went on, still not looking at her. *Where did he
go when he withdrew like this? What happened inside him?*
"It seems to me that it's time we had a little youthful
laughter around here."

His hands were cold in hers, and her stomach felt like
a hollow drum. She knew what he meant, what he was
trying to say without saying it. He was telling her to break
away—to live her own life. He would cooperate to the
extent of making an appearance Friday, but it would be a
mere formal gesture. A closing of one door and the opening
of another. He would meet the gang, and in doing so would
tactfully and tacitly release her to them.

"All right," she said. "If you like, I'll tell them to come."

"Piping-hot cheese dreams and the brown jug of hot
cocoa should fill the bill," her mother said. "Or don't you
think it will be enough?"

"Oh, heavens, Mom—plenty."

They were in the kitchen, and her mother's face was shiny with suppressed excitement as she spread the soft cheese mix over the squares of bread. "I'll pop them in the oven whenever you're ready, and they'll brown in a jiffy."

"They look wonderful, Mom." Lynn arranged the paper napkins on the sandwich tray and glanced up at the clock over the range. Her hands faltered a little. "It's after eight," she said. "Perhaps I'd better see what Dad is doing. They'll be here in a few minutes."

"All right." Her mother looked up, and the edge of worry in her eyes didn't quite match the confident smile on her lips. "Tonight won't be very easy for him, Lynn," she added, almost like a warning.

"I know. I wish I hadn't—" She set the tray on the cupboard. "I thought it might *help*, Mom." She whirled desperately. "We never have anybody. This house is like a tomb!"

"I understand, Lynn. I think your Dad understands, too. But you have to try and see it from his—well," she turned quickly back to the mixing bowl, "I think maybe we've talked enough about it, don't you? Why don't you go in and see how he's getting on?"

He was sitting in front of the low mirror, adjusting his tie. The dark suit made him look so different—so *severe*. Especially after the slacks and sloppy pullover he habitually wore.

"Hello." He spun the chair expertly on its big wheels and faced her. His eyes held the same odd uncertainty as her mother's.

"You look marvelous, Dad," she said—too quickly—and lapsed into an awkward silence. *What was there to say? What happened would just happen, that's all. . . .*

"You like my tie?" he asked, puffing it out a little. "It's new."

"It's a beautiful tie." Her hands felt like lumps of lead.

"I'm glad you like it," he smiled. "Because you gave it to me for my birthday. Remember? You said it was a party tie." His eyes grew suddenly serious. "Lynn," he said gently, "are you sure you wouldn't prefer your mother and me to stay in here? I could have caught cold, you know."

Her heart pounded and seemed to shrink at the same time. All week she had been thinking just that. And now, voluntarily, he was offering her a final escape. She could easily glaze over his absence to the gang. She would have done her part as a hostess, and the year would be stretching into spring before she would have to face the situation again.

She looked down at him. His eyes were fathomless, unreadable. Only in his fingers wrapped tightly against the tubing of the chair could she see the tension his expression concealed.

The room was so still, waiting for her to speak. To say it. But something, somewhere, was wrong. And with the swift conviction of insight she would never be able to explain, she knew.

He was frightened. But not for himself. He was frightened for her. He was afraid that he might do something awful to embarrass and hurt her in the eyes of her friends. In a way, he knew the gang better than she. If the evening didn't go well, the gang would talk about it, feel sorry for her. They would try not to let it make any difference, but it would. He was thinking of her. And she was—had been ever since she had come home filled with schemes and plans on Tuesday—thinking only of herself.

"Of course not, silly." She laughed, to cover the catch in her voice. "Why, you're the *star*. Likely as not, you'll even have to read a part. Dick Hamilton has a cold and won't be coming tonight. Would you? I mean, if we get stuck for a man?"

For a moment he just looked up at her gravely. Then, foolishly, boyishly, he grinned. "I have my script right here, Madam President," he said. He reached down into the chair and pulled out a thin volume. "*The Autumn Heart*, by Nathaniel Rogers," he read off the cover.

"Why, Dad," Lynn gasped. "That's the *play!* I mean, the one Miss Howards picked for us. How did you *know?*"

"Easy." He snapped his fingers. "I just picked up the phone this morning and called her. The library was very helpful, too. It's an interesting play. I suspect your Miss Howards knows her dramatic onions. This play is very likely to make you think."

"Is it?" Her voice seemed dangerously out of control. "None of us has read it, you know." Their eyes met, and his were alive and sparkling. Her own felt shiny, as though she were going to cry. She had never been so happy.

"Maybe I could call on you to give us an analysis of the play before we start to read it. I know the kids would like that."

"All right. If you like. But it's all here." He flipped the pages open. "In these two lines at the end of the play. It's about a man who has spent years of his life pursuing success, and suddenly he finds out what it means to love. It's a terrible shock to him. All his values go end over end. The playwright sums it up in this fragment of poetry:

> "*Love comes late to the autumn heart,*
> *But its glow is richer, like the sun*
> *Emerging from the cloudy dark. . . .*"

The silence stretched for a long moment between them.

The poetry seemed to swim against her mind, and she didn't trust herself to speak.

"I think I hear the doorbell," he said at last. "Your mother and I will come in when you're settled. All right?"

"All right." She bent swiftly and kissed his forehead.

She ran down the hall and the gang poured in on a cold rush of air. Talking and laughing, they shed scarves and coats and rubbers, and it was anyone's party at anyone's house. Only when they moved into the living room could you notice any difference at all. Sally and Madge and Carol walked down the ramp with casual unconcern. But Tommy stopped.

"Say, Mike," he said. "Look. Hey, Hig, look at this ramp. Say, that's neat, isn't it?" He looked up at Lynn with sudden embarrassment as the boys gathered around. "I mean, having it built in that way—it's a swell idea, isn't it?"

Lynn smiled. She could feel the thread of uneasiness Tommy's remark had revealed under the gang's light chatter. A few moments ago it would have terrified her. Now it was simply something that had to be broken—before it wound tight and made them uncomfortable.

"Dad calls them his private escalators." The words came. "Only he complains bitterly that he has to supply the horsepower to get up and down them."

It wasn't a good joke, but it worked. They laughed, and their relaxation was real as the boys built up the fire and the girls sorted out the manuscripts of the play.

"This is a darling room, Lynn," Madge said. "So warm, it just makes you feel at home. I suppose your father works at that desk, right there." She sighed. "It must be wonderful to just sit down and create people and places out of nothing. Gosh, I wish he would let us read *his* play sometime. That would be something."

"Say, it would," Hig chimed in. "Do you think he would, Lynn?"

For a second, her throat froze. *Had that moment in his room been real? Could it be trusted to bear the weight of such a request?* She was on the point of brightly evading, as she always had. And then she seemed to see his face as he had quoted the fragment of poetry, and it was all right. She looked at the gang. Their faces were waiting, expectant.

"Yes," she said simply. "Why don't we ask him? I know he'll say yes."

"Marvelous," Carol said. "It will really mean something to discuss a play right with the playwright himself."

"Grab chairs," Lynn said. "I'll get papers and pencils so we can start." She walked across the room with a sense of awareness of how it must look to them. It *was* warm. It wasn't a lavish and expensive room, but it had taste. It was a room that reached out to welcome you. Sometimes you had to see the familiar through a stranger's eyes to really see it at all.

In her surge of gladness and relief, she hardly noticed the hush that fell as she opened the center drawer of the desk. Then, abruptly, it engulfed her, and she turned, startled.

They were in the doorway. And again she had the odd sense of seeing, not through her own eyes, but through the eyes of the gang. They looked—well, beautiful. He was sitting so straight. He seemed to tower above the chair, reducing it to a trivial, unimportant thing. Even though her mother stood above him, something in the set of his shoulders and the lift of his chin made them seem together, as though they were standing side by side.

A second ticked by as his eyes met hers, searchingly, across the seemingly vast expanse of the room. Then he smiled.

It was as though their hands had touched. And she knew that the moment and the poem were real. Everything that had gone before was past. Somewhere, a door had closed in her mind. It was all so different. Like the man in the play whose values had been turned end over end. And now she was seeing him at last through the eyes of stranger-friends.

He *was* a cripple. He would always be imprisoned in the chair. For five years she had been fighting it, pretending it didn't exist, trying to make *him* pretend that it didn't exist because the chair was not an ennobling thing. It was real, and it had changed their lives. But it would no longer rule them. She smiled, wondering if the words were running through his mind, too.

"Like the sun, emerging from the cloudy dark. . . ."

She walked slowly across the hush of the room toward them.

"I didn't hear you come in," she said simply. She took her place beside her mother at the back of the chair, and they moved together into the room. "Gang," she said, and if her voice lifted a little with pride it was all right. He would understand. "I'd like you to meet my mother and dad."

Apron Strings

ADELE DE LEEUW

LUCY LEFT the others chattering on the high stools in front of the counter and slipped into the phone booth. She closed the door securely, dropped her nickel in the slot, and called her home number.

"Mother?"

"Yes, dear. Where are you?"

"At Barney's. The gang's talking of going out to Joe's grandfather's farm near Hamilton; his grandfather said if Joe would haul it away, he could have all the firewood he wanted, and we thought it would be fun to help Joe stock his dad's basement for winter."

Her mother said, with something of a smile in her voice, "It's lovely weather to go to the country. Who's going?"

"Oh, Bill, and Joe—we're going in his pickup truck—and Fred and Marian and Beryl and myself."

Her mother knew all of them, even Beryl. Lucy held her breath.

"It sounds crowded, but go along. You'll be home by five?"

"Oh, Mother!"

"Aunt Edna's coming for her visit, you know, and I want you to go to the station with me to meet her."

"All right," Lucy promised. It would cut things short, the gang would have fits about it—but what could she do? At least her mother hadn't objected to the outing.

She sighed with relief and opened the door. Bill turned to her with a crooked grin. "What's the verdict?"

"Okay," she said.

She hadn't thought he had even seen her go into the booth. The gang ribbed her a lot about her family. Mostly she took it in good part, but sometimes she felt that she couldn't stand another dig.

Mother and Dad were swell. They were up-to-date and good-looking, they all had fun together. But there was one flaw in them—and it was a big one. They watched over her like a couple of policemen. Oh, not too obviously, so that she squirmed. But it was bad enough. Where are you going, dear? . . . With whom? . . . What time will you be home? . . . I don't think I care to have you going to the Joint. No, that's final. . . . Do I know Kenneth? Perhaps you'd better wait till we've met him.

You'd think, to hear them, that she was too precious to be out alone. And not even alone. With the gang! They wanted to know where she was every minute. They wanted to know with whom she was; her friends had to be approved by the parental nod. It was galling to take sometimes.

Like this. When would she be home? Suppose it *was* after five—did that mean there was anything wrong? She hated having to keep track of every minute, knowing that if she didn't there would be explanations at home. And it was hard sometimes to make even the simplest matter sound simple. It hadn't struck her so forcibly, though, until Beryl Harlowe came to town. Beryl was like a breath of fresh air—she breezed into school, into their closely knit gang, into their lives. She was their own age, but years older in experience. Sophisticated, that was the word. She had her own allowance, chose her own clothes, came and went as she pleased, entertained when she felt like it, was full of plans, with no one to say her nay. It was marvelous to have her around. She was free—independent—what they all longed to be, but didn't know how to achieve. Maybe if they stayed around her enough—she was acknowledgedly their leader, even in this short time—they'd learn a thing or two.

"Let's go," said Joe, sliding off his stool. "Now that Lucy has got permission, what's holding us up?"

Beryl smiled but said nothing. Lucy felt hot inside; rebellion flared in her. This sort of thing could queer her with a girl like Beryl.

It was fun loading up the wood. They laughed and sang, and the girls climbed into the branches of a fallen tree out in the wood lot to rest, only to be driven out by the boys, who made a united assault on the unsteady hiding place. The air was winelike; it made them lightheaded and silly.

"Be sure to save all the best logs for Thanksgiving," Fred said. "We'll toast our marshmallows over 'em."

"We'll have a party at my house," Beryl said with decision. "You're all invited this minute. I know some new games; we'll have fun."

"Heave those last logs into the truck, me hearties," Joe ordered. "We have to get the princess home by five."

How did he know?

111

"Oh, gosh, there's room for more," Bill protested. "Can't we pile on those chunks over there?"

"Nope," Joe was emphatic. "It's home by five—or *else*. For Lucy, at any rate."

Muttering, but obedient, they piled into the truck again. "Keeping these logs from rolling off is going to be a job," Marian complained, as Bill swung her up into the back of the truck.

"You're supposed to hold 'em in, half-pint," Fred said. "If they go, so do you."

The truck grunted and snorted, quivered and shook— and was off. Joe put on an extra spurt of speed after glancing ostentatiously at his watch.

"Don't bite your nails, kid," he advised Lucy, who was sitting with her hands in her lap. "I'll get you there, on my honor as a Casey, if the bus holds out."

It was at that moment that the truck, hearing itself maligned, decided to quit. Cold. It wouldn't budge. Joe looked incredulous, then hurt, then worried.

"It's that load in the back," Fred said. "Bill, you better get off and walk."

"How about gas?" Marian inquired. Marian was the practical one.

"I've got plenty . . ." Joe began, and then a sheepish look spread over his face. "Oh, gosh, I mean, I thought I had. I was going to have her filled up before I left, but I forgot. . . ."

He got out and investigated. The gas tank was empty. "There's a garage about a mile and a half down the road," Bill said. "Maybe you can hitchhike."

It was Joe's truck; it was Joe's fault. "Sit tight, everybody," he said cheerfully. "I'll be back whenever you see me."

Lucy stood up and looked around. There was a farm-house not too far away.

"I—I'll go and telephone," she muttered. It was hard to get it out.

Beryl laughed. "Oh, what's the use? They won't bring gas out to anybody they don't know."

Marian explained. "She means she has to telephone home. Every hour on the hour."

"It's an old family custom," Fred contributed. "Want someone to go with you, Luce?"

"No," she said, barely above her breath.

Beryl was looking at her, practically open-mouthed. She didn't say anything. She didn't need to. Her look said it all. Incredulous. Amused. Lucy thought she saw a hint of pity, too. That was what hurt. She had dropped in Beryl's estimation—and she had been trying so hard to build herself up! The others knew about her family. They made allowances. But a girl like Beryl—what must she think? It was humiliating. She set off angrily down the road. She knew they were talking about her; she could almost hear what they said. Beryl demanding to know "what in the world?"—the others explaining with little shrugs and snickers.

"It's the last time I'll do it," Lucy thought, rebellion rising to a new height. Absolutely the last time. *Let* her parents expect it of her—she couldn't keep this up forever. After all, she was grown up.

It made it all the harder when her mother said, "Thank you for letting me know, dear. I do appreciate it."

But she clung to her resolution. She had to make her-self welcome to Beryl. To Beryl and the crowd she was draw-ing around her. Boys like Gil and Roger. Girls like Hannah and Kit. Lucy hung on the fringe, waiting for Beryl's look, her words. When Beryl included her, she was in seventh heaven. When there was something afoot, Beryl was at the root of it—something exciting, something different. And Lucy was determined not to be left out.

It took weeks to get over that trip to the country, but Beryl wasn't one to hold a thing against you too long. She really seemed to like Lucy. Lucy felt proud, elated: her self-esteem rose. It was something to be in the good graces of a girl like Beryl. She had a hard time, sometimes, keeping up with Beryl's idea of freedom, but she did her best. Relations at home were becoming somewhat difficult: her mother looked at her oddly, but said little. Her father talked to her, one evening, about her attitude, but she held her chin high and let his words slip over her consciousness.

She knew it was worth it all when Beryl stopped her in the school corridor one day.

"Lucy!" she cried hurriedly. "I've the most marvelous plan! It's super!"

"Yes?" Lucy breathed.

"We're going down to the game at Halstead next Saturday. Roger has the tickets. We'll go in Gil's car, see the game, have dinner, go to the dance, and then spend the night at Gil's uncle's apartment. We'll probably stay over Sunday, too. . . . Well, how does the plan sound to you?"

"D'you mean—you mean you want *me* to go along?" Lucy felt as if she were squeaking.

Beryl laughed. "Of course, nitwit! The four of us. I don't know of anyone I'd rather have go along. And you like Roger and Gil, don't you?"

Lucy nodded. Words absolutely failed her. It would be heavenly. Roger and Gil were boys of Beryl's caliber; they seemed older, more—well, there was that word sophisticated again, but it *did* express what she meant. They were keen about Beryl. They even seemed to like *her*. It would be wonderful to be included in that foursome. As for the weekend—if she had dreamed it up herself, she couldn't have approached it. She saw herself jumping up and down in excitement at the game, wedged between the two boys; having dinner at a little table at the inn, with candlelight making their eyes shine. She saw herself floating in Roger's and Gil's arms at the dance, meeting other boys, new ones. But even if she didn't, it wouldn't matter.

"You'll go, won't you?" Beryl, oddly enough, sounded positively anxious. Lucy felt so flattered her heart nearly burst.

"Oh, Beryl, you know how I'd love it! I'll—I'll let you know."

With those words, it was as if an icy hand fell on her. She'd have to get her parents' permission, of course, and suppose—suppose . . . But good heavens, what possible objection could they have?

She waited for a propitious moment to broach it to them. Her father had lighted one of his favorite cigars; her mother was in a glow because of something the head of the Red Cross had said to her.

"Mother—Dad . . ." she began, looking appealingly from one to the other.

And then she told them. Her eyes glistened, her breath came fast. So much, so much depended on this! She tried to make it sound just right.

A tense, strained expression crossed her mother's face. "It's out of the question. How do you feel, Jim?"

Mr. Merritt looked shocked. "Of course. It wouldn't do at all."

Lucy stared at them in abject horror. It wasn't possible —it just wasn't possible!

"But why?" she demanded hotly.

"Who is Gil's uncle?" Mrs. Merritt inquired.

"I—why, Gil's uncle."

"You don't know his name?"

"No, but I could find out."

"Is he married?"

"No, he's a bachelor."

"Would he be there? Is there anyone in the apartment other than himself?"

"He has a housekeeper, I think. Maybe he'd be there, maybe not. He travels around."

Under questioning, they brought out that the housekeeper might not be there either. She'd been ailing; she often took the weekends off.

"It wouldn't do, Lucy," Mr. Merritt said.

"You see, dear," her mother said gently, "not everybody knows you as we do. If anything happened, if you were staying in the apartment alone—the four of you—it wouldn't look right. The world has a way of talking; and the only thing to do is never give it a chance to talk."

But Lucy saw only that she was being forbidden to go. Tears failed to move them. Arguments. Everything. It wasn't the kind of party they wanted her to go on.

"You'd better let Beryl know, Luce," her father said.

Lucy sat stunned and miserable. How could she ever tell Beryl? She'd have to drag herself over there, meet Beryl's contemptuous eyes, tell her the decision, knowing that this marked the end.

She took the long way, trying to think of some way to break it that would do the least harm. But it was hopeless, however you looked at it. Beryl had freedom; *she* had none. Beryl was grown up; *she* was still considered a child. The humiliation weighed on her till she felt she couldn't bear it.

It took all her courage to ring the bell. Beryl came to the door herself. She took one look at Lucy's face.

"What's the matter?"

All the ways she had thought of breaking it deserted her. Lucy blurted out, "I can't go, Beryl."

Beryl pulled her into the living room. There was no one about; the radio was going.

"Why not?" Beryl asked curiously. "Tell me, Lucy."

Lucy sank in a chair and told Beryl what her parents had said. In her fury and hurt she left out nothing.

There was a long pause, a queer pause. Beryl said at last, "You lucky thing!"

Lucy's head jerked up. "Lucky?" she repeated stupidly.

"Lucky," Beryl said again. "I wish *I* had a family like that." Lucy had never heard that note in Beryl's voice. Wistful—young. "I'd give everything I have in the world to have a family that *cared*."

She got up and walked the length of the living room, flopped down on the couch facing Lucy. "Maybe you don't know it, but I'm tired of being on my own, doing as I please. Sometimes I don't know *what* to do, but there's nobody to ask. Mother's too busy being social. Father— Father's a sort of—remote person; I can't come close to him. They're always out. Haven't you noticed they're never here when the gang comes? They ask me sometimes, if they remember, if I had a good time wherever I was; but they don't *care* where I was."

Lucy was trying to take it in. "But I thought . . ." she hesitated.

"You thought how grand it was, didn't you?" Beryl said bitterly. "Well, it's fun for a while, but not for always. That time you had to telephone—I never knew there were people like that. You can't imagine how I envied you. The boys tease you, but they like it. You ought to be glad your parents want to know where you are and who's who and why."

Lucy said slowly, "Well, you'll have a good time without me. Any of the other girls will be thrilled . . ."

Beryl said, "But we're not going. That's off."

"Off?"

"If your parents don't like the idea of the outing, it's off," Beryl announced. "Because there must be something wrong with it."

Beryl's voice wasn't at all disappointed; it was firm and sure. She sounded glad that the decision had been made for her.

"Listen," she leaned forward tensely, "when I'm all mixed up about things, do you think I could come over sometimes and talk with your mother?"

Lucy swallowed hard. "Of course," she said. Her eyes lighted. "Why—it would be sort of like having you in the family, wouldn't it?"

Suddenly, and quite simply, she was glad, too. There would be other parties—plenty of them. The kind they could go to together. She laid her hand in Beryl's. "Why don't you come back with me right now? Dad will bring you home."

Beryl said with alacrity, "I'd love to!" She grinned at Lucy and Lucy, her heart full, grinned back. She and Beryl were on a firmer foundation now than they had ever been. She thought, with a shiver of pleasure, "I've found a real friend. And she's given me back my family."

Forbidden Yearning

MARGARET CRAVEN

WHEN THE HAND of the adjutant touched her shoulder, the girl awoke instantly and to expectancy. This was the day the work schedule changed; she was to be a bread girl again, and of all the chores, this was her favorite.

In the first gray of day, the earnest new adjutant moved softly between the long rows of cots here on the porch where the big girls slept in summer, bending now and again to awaken the others who were to work on the bread also. Then she was gone, and the girl was up and out the door, slipping down the hall to the washrooms.

Her hand found the pigeonhole which was her very own, third row right, ninth from the end. She scrubbed her teeth with the salt and the soda. She splashed cold water on her face. She soaped and washed her hands vigorously. Alone in the little room she shared with others, she dressed quickly in the dimness, and tying her work apron around her cotton frock, she hurried to the stairs to be the first one down.

In the thirteen years she had lived here, sharing Mother and Dad Dorn with two hundred and sixty brothers and sisters, Gracie Hitt had seldom known the luxury of being alone. It was only at such rare times and lately that she had come to realize that she, too, was an individual, different from all others and therefore important.

Only the night lights were burning. On the second floor there was no whisper of blanket, no rustle of sheet. The aloneness was so big she was big also, and very bold, and flinging one slim leg over the balustrade, she swooped down the last flight, landing on her soft sneakers as deft as a cat. And there in her little white nightgown, head tousled, eyes big, waited Tina Dorn.

Tina was a courtesy Dorn, having been left on the stoop, aged three days, and wrapped in a blanket. She was six now, recently moved from the nursery cottage to the main house.

"Gracie," she whispered, "is it time yet? I'm going to be a dustpan girl."

Oh, the pride of the first chore. To hold the dustpan in front of the bedroom door while the big girl who had cleaned the room swept in the litter. Gracie knew it well.

"Sh-h-h, Tina; it's hours yet. It's not 'til after breakfast." She took the hand of the little dustpan girl and they started across the entrance hall toward the front door.

To their right was the open office, and on the wall above the desk they could see poor, dear, little Gilford gazing soulfully from his dark-brown frame. Little Gilford had been the Dorns' firstborn, and all the children tried hard to feel sad that he was now an angel in heaven. Today, being bold, Gracie gave him an honest gratitude. It was little Gilford's death that had caused his parents to enter the Lord's army and accept two hundred and sixty children in his name. They had two more of their own now, and if there was any one reason why this was a home and not merely an orphanage, it was because they treated them like all the others. They ate the same food, shared the same chores, enjoyed the same treats and suffered the same punishments. If a bona-fide Dorn smacked a brother in the eye, he was exiled to the same Coventry: he had to stand in front of the main house in a pair of overalls with one brown leg and one blue leg, and take the gibes of his peers.

They came to the front door, which stood open in summer. No door was ever locked here, except, of course, the one of the closet under the stairs where the sugar and the dried fruits were stored. There were no fences, no walls. They stepped through the door onto the porch, into a day so new, so fresh that it caught the heart.

All around them were the rolling hills, the growing light glinting on the tracks where the small ones wore out the fronts of their clothes sliding down the slick dry grass on the sleds which the big boys made for them in the workshops. In the meadow under an oak grazed Dan, the old white horse, whose back was strung each afternoon with the nursery kids, their little bare heels thumping his sides to make him go faster. Beyond the grass and the flower garden near the old vineyards the gray cat was carrying the first of her new litter for safekeeping in the blackberry thicket.

But something was wrong. The little dustpan girl didn't know it yet, and the bread girl did. Almost all the children had someone, and anyone was better than no one, and they had no one. On Sunday afternoon the porch was always lined with squirming bodies and scrubbed and shining faces. And when a car turned off the dusty road and came up the drive and stopped, and out climbed the mother who had been ill, the father who had been out of work, the cousin or the aunt, something strange happened. The waiting child forgot all else—even Mother Dorn—even to say goodby to his best friend. And he went forward eagerly, yet a little shyly, with a look which was like no other.

"Why doesn't your mother ever come to see you? Don't you have anybody?" Gracie had been asked through the years. And when Tina was older, she would hear worse: "You're a foundling. You don't even have a name."

Gracie held the little hand with fierce protectiveness.

"I must go now, Tina," she said. "I have to work on the bread. Now you go back to bed. I won't forget you. I'll tell you when it's time to hold the dustpan."

They returned to the entrance hall, and the little girl scooted up the stairs, and the big girl moved quickly down the corridor to the dining room and stopped.

With the tables set for breakfast, each chair in place, each tumbler turned down, the room seemed to be waiting, hushed and eerie in the dawn, redolent of feelings and old echoes. This was the very heart of the place. Here, at Christmas, the little ones strung the paper garlands for the great tree which stood always at the far end, and the big boys carried in the piano box packed tight with dolls. Here, when she was sixteen, Gracie would receive her silver thimble, symbol of maturity.

Surely a little bit of God hovered perpetually above the ceiling, so many words had been addressed to Him here. At mealtimes the children lined up in the hall and entered, singing grace, and before leaving they stood for the hymn and knelt for the prayer.

Gracie entered slowly. It seemed to her that she could still hear her little girl's voice singing fervently her favorite hymn, "Pull for the Shore, Sailor, Pull for the Shore." And when at last the sailor was "safe in the lifeboat to sin no more," she had always been positive she had helped get him there. And she was sure now that all her life she would hear Dad Dorn giving the morning prayer, and see Mother Dorn as she stood after supper above the bowed heads of her huge family and asked that He hold every single one in the palm of His hand—and especially the bad ones.

Then why was she afraid of what she had determined to do? Was it because she was old enough to know that there are some who think faith possible only to the very young or the credulous?

She walked to the center of the huge room. She remembered having been told that when her mother brought her here, her little clothes had been clean and carefully made and hem-stitched, and this gave her confidence.

She lifted her head and she spoke boldly to the Lord. "If my mother hasn't come for me, there must be a reason," she said. "And I want her to find me, and if she cannot, I want You to help me find her, and I ask it."

She dropped the words like pebbles in a sea and, almost running, slipped among the tables into the pantry, through it and into the big kitchen and the smell of the yeast.

Cookie was standing by the stove, stirring the immense kettle of oatmeal, her cotton robe wrapped firmly around her ample middle, her face framed in kid curlers.

"Bless you, Gracie, I'm glad it's you. Now I can get these bobbins out of my hair. Have a cup of hot chocolate, child," and Cookie whacked the spoon against the side of the kettle and put it down.

"And, Gracie, don't be lifting the flour sacks by yourself. The boy will be along with the milk cart directly. And when the others come, make them wash their hands, and watch they rinse them well. I will not have my good bread tainted of soap."

Then Gracie was alone and, when she had finished her chocolate, she heard the rattle of the milk cart coming from the barn, the boy singing as he pushed it, and she knew then he was Carl.

He came up the back steps and through the door, eager as the new day, a fine-looking lad in his worn blue overalls, sleeves rolled high on big strong arms. He saw her and stopped.

"Good morning, Gracie," he said shyly.

"Good morning, Carl."

He took the knife from his pocket and opened it, and he cut the chain stitch on the first flour sack carefully because it must be washed and bleached and used. He lifted the sack, Gracie ready at the bread table, and, as he began to pour, she raised the board which dammed the yeast mixture into the three-foot trough and let it trickle through the softly falling flour.

There was a difference between them. Carl had a family. Carl belonged to people, and they to him. When his mother had died, his father had refused to separate the six children and brought them to the home, and he had found work nearby so he could see them frequently, and each month he had contributed toward their care.

When Carl had finished pouring the flour into the trough, Gracie dipped in her hands to begin the mixing.

"My father is coming this Sunday, Gracie," he said. "We are going to take my brothers and sisters on a picnic. If you will come with us, I will ask Mother Dorn's permission. My father says he will be pleased to have you."

Something big and bold within her answered. "Thank you, Carl, but I'm expecting to see my mother," and for an instant his face was empty of expression, so tightly did he contain his doubt.

"Some other time, Gracie," he said, and he put away his knife and left the kitchen quickly, whistling.

When the three other bread girls straggled in, Gracie made them wash their hands and rinse them. Now there were eight hands working the yeast into the flour, until it was smooth and spongy and ready for the raising.

After breakfast, Gracie remembered to tell Tina when the moment arrived to hold the dustpan proudly and without a wiggle. Yet already she was waiting for her answer. In midmorning, when she returned to the kitchen to help knead and shape the loaves, the dough seemed almost alive, and she pushed it hard with the heels of her palms, lifted and turned it deftly until it pushed back at her. And in the afternoon, when the big and middle girls gathered under the trees to mend socks, to shell peas into the huge dishpans, and they sang the old songs—"Juanita" and "Swing Low, Sweet Chariot"—Gracie forgot her turn to pick up the refrain, so big was the dream within her.

She held tight the dream, though she knew it was child-ish. It had been her companion on many a night through the years. To it she had given infinite variation. Now she added another. She added Tina; she and Tina would be waiting on the porch with the scrubbed and eager ones of a Sunday afternoon. Into the drive would turn a long and shining car, its back seat bulging with treats for all the kids, and when it stopped, out would step such a mother as the children's home had never seen—so blond, so lovely—

"Gracie, you're woolgathering," said the adjutant. "You're a thousand miles away. Come back here," and Gracie shut off the dream and picked up the refrain, and wove another thread into the heel of some small boy's sock.

Gracie felt an instant's fear. Oh, she must be careful of

this new green adjutant with the pretty face. But the fear did not come again. That evening when the adjutant was in charge of putting the smallest ones to bed in the nursery cottage, Gracie helping her, it was obvious no dumber help had ever been sent by the Lord to the children's home.

Even the two-year-olds knew it. When they knelt in the nursery for the "Lay-me-down" and the "God-blessing," it looked for a time as if the hated moment of climbing into the cribs was going to be postponed for hours, if not indefinitely.

They God-blessed all the brothers and the sisters and the help, and were working their way optimistically toward the pussy cats, the puppy dogs, the woolly worms and the garter snakes, when the adjutant sent a frantic appeal for help above their heads.

"That'll be enough of that," said Gracie loudly and cheerfully. "Just God-bless everything and everybody in all the world and that will do it. . . . Now does anybody want a drink? . . . Does anybody have to go to—" And the small ones knew they were licked, and permitted themselves to be tucked in, and the adjutant sent Gracie a look of respect and thank-you.

While she waited, Gracie found it harder and harder to keep her mind on the chores, even the pleasant ones at playtime.

On doughnut night, when the big girls took turns dropping the sweet rings into the hot, deep fat, Gracie was so busy with her dream that she let her batch grow too brown on the edges, and even Cookie looked at her strangely.

And one afternoon when Dad Dorn took some of the middle ones down the dusty road to the river to teach them to swim, Gracie sat so absentmindedly on the bank, and held the rope so carelessly that the child dog-paddling at its end floundered just a little, and Dad Dorn had to yell at her loudly, "Gracie, pull him in!"

She avoided Mother Dorn's wise and gentle eyes. Each Thursday night after bedtime, Mother Dorn came upstairs to discuss with her daughters the problems suitable to each age group. Sometimes she brought her guitar, and when all the questions had been asked and answered, she sang to them. Gracie asked no questions. When Mother Dorn sang "Kiss Me Again, Little Darling," which was her favorite, she kept her face turned away, afraid she might meet those eyes and lose her dream by telling it. And once when Mother Dorn said, "Good night, Gracie," in her gentle voice, Gracie even pretended to be asleep.

Yet each Sunday Gracie avoided the porch where the children awaited their visitors. She kept Tina close to her, and they would sit under the trees, apart from the others, and watch the porch until even Tina looked at her a little anxiously.

On bread days, when Gracie hurried to be the first one down, and entered the eerie dining room, she did not remind Him of her request, determined to prove she could wait patiently.

Carl did not question her. One morning, lifting the heavy sack to pour the flour into the trough, he said, "I'm going to be a doctor, Gracie. I'm going to start working toward it right now. I'm going to ask Dad Dorn to help me. What are you going to be?"

"I don't know. I haven't decided. I haven't even thought of it," and she let the yeast mixture trickle so fast into the flour that it splashed.

"You could be a nurse," Carl said. "Mother Dorn would help you. We might work together. We might come back here to the home and work. Some kids do."

"I don't know," she said quickly and almost resentfully.

127

"I don't want to talk about it," and this was strange, since she liked Carl.

One day the green new adjutant sought out Mother Dorn, her pretty face worried.

"It's about Gracie Hitt," she said. "I'm worried about her. She's such a bright girl."

"Yes-s-s."

"It's as if she's waiting for something. On Sundays when visitors come, she hangs around the front porch where the children are gathered. She never goes up on the porch to wait with them. She stays under the trees in the yard with Tina. There's a special bond between those two— something lasting. They're closer than sisters."

"They are the two who have no one of their own," said Mother Dorn slowly.

"I know that, but it's strange nevertheless. On bread mornings Gracie is always the first one down. You know where I think she goes? Into the dining room. It's so quiet then and sort of scary. It's not good for her. Why?"

"If your mother had brought you here when you were very small and left you and never came back, wouldn't you wonder why? And when you grew older, wouldn't you hope and pray she'd come? And if she did not, wouldn't you try and find her?"

"You mean she'll run away?"

"I mean she'll remember everything she can of the home she once had, and seek a chance to return and search for it. Since it was in a town only sixty miles distant, it should be fairly easy for her to begin her search."

"But you don't mean you'll let her? Suppose she should find her mother. There's no telling what kind of woman she may be."

"Have you so little faith?" asked Mother Dorn.

Meanwhile Gracie waited and had no answer. Oh, it was obvious what was wrong. Dad Dorn was right when he said at prayer that the Lord loves those who help themselves. On the sleeping porch in the quiet night, she tried hard now to remember her life before her mother had brought her here. The memories were few and vague. Only a few stood out.

She could remember the time her mother had come into the kitchen with an apronful of baby chicks, and she had squealed with delight and reached for them, and her mother had said, "Be careful. You'll hurt them." There was a toy monkey on a stick. There were open shelves at one end of the kitchen where the cookie crock stood. The wooden house had stood on a hill—an old gingerbread house with an ornate porch. If the house still stood, she was sure she could find it in the hot valley town whose name she remembered.

Each afternoon, in the sewing room, older girls worked on the boys' shirts, and for this they were paid. Gracie asked Mother Dorn if she might work also, and Mother Dorn asked no questions and agreed.

No one worked so carefully to keep the seams straight, to make such fine buttonholes. When Mother Dorn inspected Gracie's first shirt and told her she had done well, Gracie could not meet her eyes. It was a rule in the home that if you had a problem, you took it straight to Mother or Dad Dorn, and she had not done so.

In two weeks she had saved enough money to buy a bus ticket to the valley town of her childhood, and the very next Saturday she had a chance to get away. It happened so naturally that Gracie could only consider it providential, and it seemed to her appropriate that providence had used for its instrument the green new adjutant.

Each Saturday morning the adjutant went to town to shop, and sometimes she asked a middle or an older girl to accompany her and help with the errands and the packages. This time she asked Gracie.

Gracie sat beside her in the ancient pickup in which they would carry home the supplies. In her pocket, wrapped in a handkerchief, was the money she had earned. She clutched it tightly, trying to hide her eagerness and to be natural. But the adjutant was so dumb that she noticed nothing, and the supermarket was so full of shoppers that escape was easy.

While the adjutant plucked cans from the shelves, Gracie slipped into the crowded aisle, around a corner into another and out. She knew where the bus station was, and she ran all the way, holding tightly to the handkerchief with the money, so breathless that, when she arrived, she could scarcely ask for a ticket.

Only eight minutes to wait, and the bus already loading, and so crowded it was easy to make herself inconspicuous in a rear seat, hidden by the latecomers who had to stand.

When the bus started, Gracie pretended to be tying her shoe. She was afraid to look up. The adjutant must have missed her by now, and might be scuttling on the street like a frightened chicken. But when the bus reached the outskirts of the small town, she straightened and felt safe, freedom and daring like a wind in her face.

The bus stopped at every crossroads. People climbed off and people climbed on, and the driver had to help stow their luggage. When it reached the town of her early childhood it was almost noon, and she spent a precious dime for a glass of milk, swallowing it quickly because she was eager to begin her search.

It was little more than a village, dusty and hot in the summer sun, a cluster of old stores, and three roads leading out. In each store she sought the oldest employee and asked each if he had heard the name Hitt. No one had.

Each of the three roads led upward toward hills terraced with grapevines. She chose one, trudging along sturdily. But the houses were all new, set far back among trees, and this could not be right, so she returned and tried the second road. It was no better. Nothing was familiar. Not a bend. Not a tree; so, after following the road for a mile or so, she retraced her steps.

When she started on the third road, she was almost without hope. She was tired and she was hungry, and her feet dragged. There were new houses set back among trees, and they were wrong, and then there was a half mile or so with no houses at all. And then a small old white house, and the road began to climb. And suddenly it seemed to Gracie that her feet knew the way, knew the bend was there before her eyes saw it, knew the clump of trees would be waiting to the right.

Her steps quickened and suddenly she forgot her weariness. And then she saw it. She saw the house at the top of the hill. It had been long neglected, the fence unmended, the gate hanging on one hinge. It was a wooden house, a gingerbread house, with an ornate porch, and somebody lived in it, because washing hung on a line at the rear.

This is the house, something told her. *This is the house.* And she was afraid to go on, and determined to go on, and she walked through the gate and up the path, and she climbed the shabby steps to the door.

She knocked and waited. From somewhere in the rear of the house came the faint sound of voices, querulous, dulled by old quarrels. Gracie knocked again, more insistently, and the voices stopped, and a woman said, "I'll see who it is," and steps came to the door. It opened.

"What do you want, kid?" asked the woman, and Gracie searched the dull, worn face for some faint sign of recognition, and her eyes swept past the woman, down the hall to the kitchen, and found the open shelves where the cookie crock had stood. She was sure of the house then, and this gave her courage.

"I lived here once when I was very small," she said. "I lived here with my mother. She took me to the children's home and she never came back for me, and I'm trying to find her."

The woman stared. For an instant something flickered in her eyes and went out.

"You must know something. The name's Hitt—Gracie Hitt."

The woman said almost indolently, "Never heard it. We ain't lived here too long. Our name's Lombrosi. You can see it on the mailbox by the tree. Lombrosi's our name."

From the rear of the house a man's voice asked, "Who is it?"

The woman went quickly down the hall. "Just some kid. I'll get rid of her," and shut the door. Then she came back.

"Sorry I can't help you," she said. "You been living at the orphanage, you say? They good to you there?"

"Oh, yes!"

"They feed you good?"

"Yes, they do."

"Well, if I hear anything about the Hitts, I'll let you know. Not likely." Then there was a silence and, as Gracie turned to go, the woman took a step forward.

"Your mother'd be mighty proud to have a nice girl like

you," she said. "She'd be mighty proud. You remember that, kid," and she started to close the door.

Gracie walked down the steps and the path. At the gate she looked back. The door was open just a crack and the woman was watching her. Then it shut with a click.

Gracie walked slowly back to the village, possessed by a huge and aching doubt. She waited on the battered bench at the bus stop, unable either to accept or to discard. On the bus trip back, she scarcely thought at all, only felt.

But when at last the ride was over and she was walking the last quarter mile on the road to the children's home, for the first time she realized she had run away. She had left without permission. No girl had ever been sent to Coventry, made to stand in front of the main house in a pair of overalls with one blue leg and one brown leg. She would be the first. She would suffer it gladly just to get home. She would accept it cheerfully, and more, too—even the words Mother Dorn would surely speak, and which she deserved.

She could hardly wait to reach the place in the road from which she could see the tracks on the hills where the small ones coasted their sleds down the dry grass, and when she reached it, she saw also Dad Dorn waiting in the road with a bunch of kids, and one of them cried, "Here she comes!"

They came to meet her.

"Gracie child," Dad Dorn said, "we're so glad you're home. We've been watching for you," and he put his hand on her shoulder, the kids tagging along, playing games as they went.

He did not question her. He did not ask where she had been. When they came to the main house, he said,

133

"Cookie's saved your dinner, Gracie. Now run along. You must be starved."

It was so late now that the nursery kids were in their cots, the small ones going up to bed. The kitchen was empty and the dishes done, and Gracie's dinner was warm on the back of the big stove.

She ate slowly because she knew what she must do, and she both wanted and dreaded it. Then she walked through the dining room and down the long corridor to the office and knocked.

Poor dear little Gilford was gazing from his frame, and at the desk sat Mother Dorn.

"I'm glad you've come, Gracie," she said gently. "I knew you would. I've been waiting for you."

And Gracie sat down in the chair by the desk and told her everything. She spilled it out, holding back nothing, and Mother Dorn did not interrupt or question her. When she had finished, there was silence.

"I was so sure He would answer me," said Gracie.

"But didn't He?"

"Yes, I suppose—yes, I—"

"You are sorry you went?"

"No. Only"—and now she came to the part that hurt most—"only now I'll never know. I'll never be sure if she is my mother or is not."

"But you're sure of the thing that counts. If this woman is your mother, she brought you because she felt you would find here a better chance in life than she could give you. And if this is true, surely there are times when the love of giving up is greater than the love of keeping."

For a moment, Mother Dorn was busy with some papers on her desk.

"Carl's father is taking his family to the circus next Saturday," she said. "Carl has asked permission to take you and Tina. Tina's never been to a circus. Tina has no one, Gracie. I have hoped you would be her sister."

"But I am—I mean I feel I am. I'll take her. I'd love to take her. If she gets too tired, I'll see she rests. I'll be careful of her."

"I'll let you tell Carl, Gracie. A huge box of clothes came in today, and I've picked a new dress for you to wear, and one for Tina. Tomorrow we'll talk further. We've had enough excitement for one day. Off to bed with you, child."

She went with Gracie to the door, and opened it on a surprising sight. Tina was going up the stairs, the adjutant after her. Tina was holding up her little white nightgown, and under it she had on her bloomers, both legs bulging. Cookie had forgotton to lock the storage closet, and Tina was taking a treat for the kids in the small girls' ward.

"Tina," said Mother Dorn, and Tina turned quickly, and the bloomer elastics broke, and she stood there raining old dried prunes all over the stairs. And the adjutant burst into laughter, and Mother Dorn also.

"Oh, what a family I have," said Mother Dorn.

When the prunes were picked up, Gracie undressed in her little room, and slipped into her cot on the sleeping porch. She lay still in the dark, and she put down her old dream of the car coming up the drive. She put it down tenderly, as one puts away a doll, a monkey on a stick, a toy much loved in childhood.

Tomorrow was bread day. She could hardly wait for it to come. She would be the first one down. She would tell Carl she would go to the circus and she would thank him.

"When I grow up, I think maybe I'll be a nurse," she would say.

135

And when he had poured all the flour into the trough and put away his knife and gone, she would mix the yeast into the flour. She would mix it until it was spongy, and knead it until the dough pushed back at her.

In her mind the bread dough was life, and Gracie Hitt held her life now in her own two hands.

Gather Ye Rosebuds

MARION DOW

"EMILY?" Mary Gorman called anxiously from the shadowy lower hall.

"Yes, Mama?"

"Emily, it's seven o'clock. The ladies will be here any minute now."

"Yes. Mama?"

"What?"

"May I use your bath salts, Mama?"

"I said yes this afternoon. Call down when you want me to zip you up."

"I can manage."

"No, you call." There was a pause; then, "You feel all right, Emily?"

"Yes. Yes, I feel all right."

But she didn't, Emily thought weakly. She locked the bathroom door and leaned against it, closing her eyes and

137

shivering despite the warm May evening and the stuffiness of the little bathroom with its old-fashioned white tub set high on four small white lion's paws. She ran the hot water into the tub; the pipes gurgled and spat the first pint viciously.

She sat down on the low white stool and waited patiently. Seven o'clock . . . probably nine before he came for her . . . another three and a half hours until twelve-thirty, at which hour she must be home. Five and a half hours until she could undress and lie down on her narrow bird's-eye maple bed and be swallowed up in peace, security, aloneness and sleep.

Or, she thought, looking up at the damp-stained ceiling, she could recall what might prove to be sheer magic. She was sixteen, and this was her first date.

"Time enough," Mama had said so often. "Time enough for boys."

"But Ellamay . . ." Emily would protest faintly.

"And don't you Ellamay me, Emily Gorman. Her mother doesn't care who she goes out with, with her bragging 'Ellamay went here' and 'Ellamay's going there.' You mark my words, one of these fine days Ellamay will be parading down the church aisle with the wrong man. They'll be old before they're twenty, these girls. You stay young as long as you can, I say. And if you think I'm going to lie awake at night wondering where you are and . . ."

"There aren't many places I could be in Forest Lake. Jen's amusement room—or Hilda's—playing ping-pong or dancing or something."

"Yes," Mary Gorman would nod knowingly. "Something. I know this something."

So Emily hadn't asked any more. For a year and a half she had grown accustomed to hearing the girls say: "No use asking Emily. *She* can't go."

138

Or: "Honestly, Emily, you'll just grow up to be an old maid!"

Or Ellamay, who was braver than the rest, would declare: "If I had a mother like yours, Emily, I'd just *tell* her. Or I'd get on a bus to the city and get a job. Just because *she's* sour on life . . ."

But there, of course, Emily always had to come to Mama's defense. Because there were things about Mama she knew in her heart that could not be told in the high school gymnasium locker room, or in the echoing halls on the way to classes.

Emily sprinkled the blue salts sparingly on the water and swished her hand around. Hyacinth, it said on the bottle. She turned off the tap, slipped off the blue cotton robe and put one foot down experimentally, then slid down into the warm water.

The evening still held the elements of dreamlike unreality: that Mama had consented and that Howard Stewart had asked her. She knew him as one of her class, admired his tennis and basketball and swimming, admired even more his scholastic accomplishments; next year he would enter college to study nuclear physics. Once, more than a year ago, he had asked her to a football game, but of course she could not go. He probably knew about Mama's rules, for this time he had prefaced his invitation, "Emily, do you think your mother would let you go with me to the class dance?"

It had taken Mama two month-long days to consent. Doubtless she had been influenced by those mothers in her Ladies' Friendly Society who, having daughters of their own, found courage to speak their minds to Mary Gorman over the hems while sewing for orphans.

"It's a shame, that's what it is, Mary Gorman, not allowing that pretty little thing loose from your apron strings. How do you expect she's ever going to know how to behave, or find herself a nice young man when the time comes?"

Mama would snort, "The time hasn't come."

"Why!" said gaunt, angular Jessie Schmitt, "I was married when I was eighteen. Jen was born before I was twenty."

"Yes," Mary Gorman would say coldly. "Yes, I know." And she might very well have added, except that they all knew it, but not as Emily knew it: "So was I."

Married and pregnant, deserted, a mother . . . in that order, Emily thought sadly, with a distrust and hatred for George Gorman and all his sex that had put bitterness on her tongue these many years.

"I want something better for you," she would sometimes say to Emily, as in the winter they sat, one on each side of the round living room table—Mama with her sewing, because her trade as a seamstress was what sustained them, and Emily with her books.

Emily got out of the bath and rubbed herself briskly on the rough snow-white towel. She looked at herself critically in the steam-blurred mirror. She had just begun to acquire a summer tan, but tonight she was pale, and the brown eyes under the straight brows were troubled. She had never been allowed to have any illusions about herself. "Pretty is as pretty does," Mama always said. "Don't go getting ideas. You'll pass."

But Mama had taken pains with the dress, on her knees endlessly pinning, basting, bending over the tiny tucks in the pale pink voile hour after hour. Secretly Emily had hoped for a "bought" dress, but of course that was not to be contemplated. And it *was* a pretty dress, narrow-waisted, wide flaring skirt and three-quarter sleeves. Mama didn't approve of off-the-shoulder immodesty.

Back in her room, Emily heard the doorbell ring. The Ladies' Friendly! It was altogether unfortunate that this had to be their night to sew here, because it meant they would look her over, with their eyes sharp as needles sticking into her from her brown head to the tips of her white slippers, and she would shrivel up before Howard—Howie —she must remember to call him Howie—ever came.

Her fingers were awkward as she dressed, and she thought wistfully of Jen and Ellamay and Hilda, in a gay confusion of expectancy, punctuated with many telephone calls to each other to check on every detail.

"Are you wearing your blue tonight, or your yellow?"

"I simply don't know whether I should take my *good* coat or a scarf. What would *you* do?"

Emily hoped such a call might come for her, although it was unlikely. The pink voile was her only party dress. There was no alternative. Happily, the evening was very warm. She would be saved the necessity of wearing her dark brown coat, or the knitted scarf Mama insisted she carry.

Her nervousness and countless uncertainties should have brought some bright flush to Emily's cheeks, but the sad truth was that she looked less attractive than usual, colorless. Her chances of applying rouge surreptitiously from the compact she had bought a week ago, and then running the gauntlet of Mama's Ladies' Friendly (to say nothing of passing under Mama's sharp black eyes) gave little hope of its use; and once in Howard's—Howie's—company, it would be awkward and impossible.

Delaying as much as she could in dressing, turning this way and that to look at herself in the dim mirror, standing in stocking-feet on the chair to see the hem of the skirt that was, she knew, much too long . . . still, with all this, she was completely dressed and ready at eight o'clock. Perspiration beaded her forehead. Her hands and feet were like ice.

"Mama?" she called softly down the stairs, through the rising chatter of women's voices. "Mama?"

Mary Gorman hurried to peer up the stairway.

"Yes, Emily?"

"Will you zip my dress up, please, Mama?"

"Coming. Coming." She heard Mama's breathless apology for a short absence, then Mama was there, pulling up the zipper, patting the little tucks, saying, "Well, I must say it looks very nice on you, Emily; you needn't feel ashamed. These bought things, they're put together with nothing but basting. But this . . . no. Emily, stand up straight; put your shoulders back. You look all flat here— a nice shape you would have if you stood right."

"Oh, Mama, don't fuss so, *please*." Tears filled her eyes; she dashed them away angrily, stifling a sob.

"*Now*, what's wrong?"

"I don't know. I just wish it was over. I won't do the right things. I know I won't. I don't know how to act at these things, Mama. If you'd let me go out once in a while like Jen or Ellamay—"

Mary Gorman's face hardened. "What is this? What does this Ellamay have that you don't have? Tell me, now!" Angrily, she forced the words out.

"Well . . ." desperately, "*something*. I don't even know how to talk to boys, Mama. I'm—I don't think I'm well. I'm hot, then I'm cold. I wish I was dead!"

"Such talk," Mama snorted. "This was your idea. You wanted to go," she reminded coldly.

Emily rushed on. "Yes, I know. I did. I *do*. You never wanted me to go out with boys and I feel now as though you were . . . *pushing*." Emily covered her hot, tear-stained face. "I'll do all the wrong things and no one will ever ask me again."

"Stop that!" Mama said curtly. "If you want to begin, then begin. You let him do the talking. They always talk about themselves."

"Yes, but Howard—Howie is smart, Mama. He's an honor student."

"That makes him different? He'll talk about himself. Emily, if you want to marry one day," she said sternly, "then you must learn, learn a lot. If you listen enough, maybe you'll learn."

Mary Gorman went out of the room, closing the door firmly.

Emily sat down on her bed, her head dizzy with confused thoughts. She hadn't been able to say what she meant. Because all mixed up with Emily's fear of not knowing what to say—of lacking social niceties and the bold casualness she envied, observed in others—was a rising panic in her breast, increasing as the hour of nine became more imminent, at the thought of Howard Stewart's hand on her arm, around her waist. Would he want to kiss her good night? She hoped he would, and at the same time hoped he wouldn't. And why she had ever hoped to convey all this to Mama she did not know.

She should be happy and singing; her eyes should be shining. Noting it was only eight-thirty—how could time be paradoxically so swift and so terribly slow?—she turned off the light over her bureau, went to the open window and being very careful of her dress, knelt on the floor, her chin on the rough sill.

A faint glow of departing sunset stained the west gold beyond the maples along the street. A planet she could not name hung with blue fire in the southern sky. She heard a

143

mother calling children in from play, and there was an owl in Mr. Friehof's orchard. The fragrance of linden trees in bloom came in on the soft evening air, and she closed her eyes and breathed deeply. From far off came the poignant, lacerating whistle of a train, piercing and prolonged. And suddenly the night, the fragrance, the uncertainties, the pain of Mama's private fears and torments—all became unendurable, and she wished that there might be a passage through the Red Sea of youth into the old age that must be blessedly exempt from yearning and growing and this hard instruction.

"Emily!"

She got up, brushed the tears from her eyes and re-examined herself in the mirror.

"Emily, come down so the ladies can see your dress."

She went down; she turned obediently while ten pairs of eyes moved, razor-like, from her white slippers to the top of her shining brown head. They said all the pretty, complimentary things that made Emily feel now hot and now cold. They chattered like sparrows at a feast, recalling their own first dates with abandoned delight.

Emily sat down on the piano bench. Nine o'clock. Twenty past, half-past nine. Before ten o'clock Emily went upstairs twice to the bathroom. At ten-fifteen she did not come down again. She heard Mama getting refreshments, coffee, ice cream and cake, and the muted voices, funereal, conveying shock and disbelief.

What were young people coming to, they demanded, going out so late? And there followed advice to Mary Gorman about speaking firmly to the young man . . . *when* he came.

When, at ten-forty-five, it became all too apparent that Howard Stewart was not coming at all, their strident indignation rose with their final good nights.

Emily, not able to unzip her dress, lay down in it on the bed and wept sick tears of shame into the faded blue coverlet. She was as tired as though she had danced all night; her muscles ached with strain; the shock of rejection lay like a dreary illness over her mind.

Mama finally came up, after eleven o'clock. She unzipped the pink dress with one rough, downward gesture, and from her thin lips she let flow a flood of abuse, searing and painful.

"Well! Now you see! Pigs, that's what they are; dogs, the whole lot of them. And don't tell me some of them are different. They'll break a woman's heart with no by-your-leave. And you might as well learn it sooner as later."

Emily stood, hands pressed over her ears, tears running down her cheeks, the discarded dress encircling her feet.

"Mama, no. *No!* Stop it, Mama. I won't listen."

"You'll listen. What do you suppose all those women are saying? Emily Gorman is jilted! Maybe because her mother takes in sewing, and Emily doesn't have the right clothes? And this boy—this honor student—does he call you up and say 'Pardon me'? Do they ever? No. You can sit and sit and sit, and are supposed to smile and say thank you for nothing, for what they throw at you."

The words dropped like pure vitriol, all Mary Gorman's life's defeats and ignominy focused now in ugly abuse. And it was this thought suddenly that penetrated the girl's misery as she stood, trembling, tearful and shocked.

She dropped her hands from her ears and stepped out of her dress, picked up her blue cotton robe from the bed and covered her shaking body.

"Stop it, Mama," she said with new authority. "I won't listen to you. And I won't grow up believing all this that you say is true."

"It's true all right. What more do you want to start off

with?" Mary Gorman thrust forward her blotched, angry face. "It's true."

"Maybe for you, yes. For me, no. I can't grow up believing this," the girl repeated. "There's so much *beauty* in the world, Mama—" her voice broke as she recalled those moments earlier by the window when some of the magnificence of the night, of being alive to live it and breathe it in, penetrated to her.

"That's what I'm going to believe, to hold to, Mama," and in this moment she recognized the separation from this woman who was her mother, and her inability to reach across the gulf and convey what she felt, what she meant: the fragrance of the spring night, of the linden trees in bloom, the owl, and the star, and even the loneliness of that train moving through the night to a fixed, far destination. No, there weren't words. Or if there were, they could not be spoken now to her mother.

Mary Gorman turned a brusque shoulder, snatched the dress from the floor and threw it viciously on the bed. "We'll see! We'll just see about that!" she hissed.

"I don't think you knew what was going to happen tonight, Mama," Emily said, her voice quiet. "But I believe you're glad it happened. Oh, Mama!" Emily cried, overcome with overwhelming pity and compassion for her mother.

"Oh, Mama," said Emily again. "Go now. Go to bed." With new gentleness, "Go to bed, now."

And Mary Gorman went out and closed the door.

Emily undressed; she washed her face, turned back her bed, and in her nightgown and robe she knelt by the open window, laid her head on her arms and quietly, silently wept. But not for herself.

Into her long communion came the faint sound of the

146

telephone bell ringing in the lower back hall. She went down, barefoot in the dark, wondering and hurrying.

"Emily? Is that you, Emily?" came Howard Stewart's voice.

"Yes. Yes," she said, barely above a whisper.

"Well, I'm certainly glad it's you. I thought maybe your mother would answer and she wouldn't call you. Emily, I just bribed the nurse to let me have a phone here because I just had to—"

"Nurse? Howie—what—how?"

"Oh, it's all right; I broke a collarbone. It's nothing serious, really. But you see, I was out like a light, and of course everyone was too busy and too stupid to think of calling you. They were busy, hovering, you know, you can imagine. And just saying I'm sorry sounds stupid, but—"

"But you mustn't think about it, Howard—Howie—I just knew something must have—"

"I'm groggy and don't sound right, I know. But it was all tiresome. When I went down the back steps to the garage, like a dolt I fell over something. It was stupid," he repeated. "So long as you understand, Emily?"

"Oh, I do; I *do*. Of course I do."

"When I get out of here, I'll come around right away and explain to your mother. Emily?"

"Yes?"

"The nurse says I have to hang up now."

"Yes, of course. You let them take care of you, Howie."

"Good night. Thanks, Emily. I figured you'd be understanding."

"Thank *you*. Oh, thank *you*," said Emily softly. "Good night."

At the foot of the stairs she looked up. Her mother was standing on the upper landing, the light behind her, hair down her back.

"And who was that at this hour?"

Emily stood still, one bare foot on the lowest step.

"Just Howie, Mama." The name came quite easily. She heard her mother's indrawn breath.

"He had an accident. He broke his collarbone and he's in the hospital. He just called to say he was sorry. So you see, Mama—"

Mary Gorman said nothing. She retreated into her own bedroom, and Emily went upstairs.

In her room she turned on the light, took her diary from the drawer of the small table next to her bed, and turned to the date.

The page was white, unmarked, empty.

With her pencil Emily began slowly to write: *It has been a most beautiful day.* . . .

A Family Affair

JEAN KINKEAD

I F YOU read any of those music magazines, maybe you saw
the picture of Sue Hall (that's my girl) bringing down
the Hamilton High auditorium singing "Reckon I'm in
Love," with Billy Freeman's band. The picture doesn't do
justice to Sue, with her brown-satin hair and those dark,
cocker-spaniel eyes, but it sort of brings into focus all the
excitement of that night. Billy Freeman used to go to
Hamilton, as you probably know, and when he and his
band came back to play for our Junior Prom, well, as far
as I'm concerned, it was New Year's Eve and your first
big date and everything stupendous all rolled into one.

He put on a very informal singing contest inviting anyone who hankered to sing with a band to step up to the
mike, and they were all pretty funny. The boys were red-
faced and hoarse, the girls nervous and giggly. All, that is,
but my girl. Sue has all kinds of poise—caught, no doubt,

149

from her speech-making mother, who has a finger in every civic pie in town. But as for baking a devil's-food cake for her daughter every now and then, or inviting a guy to Sunday night supper—heck, no!

I've known for a long time how Sue wished her Mom were less of an institution and more of a Mom. I've heard it in her voice sometimes, like on her birthday when her mother was in Boston at some kind of a meeting. Sometimes it's in her eyes, as when she got the lead in Junior Night, and she dashed home to tell the family, and nobody was there. Anyway, Sue stood in front of the mike, her hands clasped loosely in front of her, and she sang in a clear, sure, smiling voice that made the back of my neck tingle.

"Is it just me?" I remember wondering. "Or is she terrific?"

And then everyone began clapping and the boys whistled through their teeth, and Billy came over and put his arm around her and asked her to sing again. To make a long story short, Sue won the contract, and the prize was to sing with the Freeman band the Saturday it opened at New York's Paramount Theater.

I walked home with her after the prom, feeling like Mr. Lana Turner or somebody and not sure that I liked the feeling. "Will you come and listen to me, Johnny?" she asked. "If you and Mom and Daddy and Cynnie and Joe aren't all in the very front I absolutely won't be able to bear it."

"The Sue Hall Fan Club will be out in full force," I told her.

Then, feeling that the chatter about singing had gone on long enough, I began talking about baseball, and Hamilton's gift to same (that's me), and we were almost at her gate when I realized that she hadn't been listening at all.

"I wonder what I'll wear?" she was saying. "Maybe my yellow check . . ." And when I kissed her good night, which is usually fun, it was like kissing my grandmother.

All the way home I was thinking in an irked sort of way, "Gee, her singing isn't *really* so red-hot," and I was wishing Billy Freeman and his almighty band would drop dead.

I was at her house the Saturday the letter came from Billy Freeman's agent saying the booking was all set. They were opening on the seventeenth, and would she be on hand for the matinee show. If she got there at one, there'd be time for a rehearsal before they went on. There was a check for $50 enclosed to pay for her dress and traveling expenses. She jumped up and down like someone aged two.

Her father, who's Hamilton's athletic coach and not known as a comedian, looked at me and shifted his pipe to the other side of his mouth. "Move over, Kirsten Flagstad," is what I think he said.

I guess I laughed a little too loud for his paternal pride, because the next time he glanced over at me, he looked as if I'd just made the third out with Hamilton's bases full.

Sue's mother was typing something at her desk, and she didn't say anything at all for a minute, just glanced up with a funny expression on her face and pushed the space bar on the typewriter up and down a couple of times. "The seventeenth?" she said finally.

Sue reread the letter. "Saturday the seventeenth at one o'clock," she read in a sort of singsong, and then she spun around, waving her check, and kissed her father's nose. "Turn in your gym suit," she told him. "We're rich."

"The seventeenth," Mrs. Hall was saying, "is the day of that luncheon. Saturday the seventeenth at one o'clock. . . ."

Sue's lively face went dead. "Well, that's okay, isn't it?" she said, speaking too quickly and too loudly. "I mean, you don't have to come to hear me."

"I think you miss the point," Sue's father said. "It's just possible that your mother would like to have her children around her at that luncheon."

I guess they'd forgotten all about me standing there looking from one to the other like someone watching a three-man ping-pong game. I withdrew to the screened-in porch. I knew all about the luncheon Sue's mother was talking about. Mrs. Hall had been named Mother of the Year by some group or other, and they were having this big feed for her over at the Woman's Club.

"Oh, but *Mother*," Sue almost whispered. "You wouldn't make me—"

"Make you," her father boomed, in the same voice he used when a guy fouls a clean pitched ball. "Why—"

"James!" Mrs. Hall cut the word off so short that it didn't hang in the air a split second but, brother, did old man Hall shut up. "Of course, I wouldn't make you go, Susie," she said. "There are some things only our hearts can decide for us."

"I know I won't be able to make this sound the way I mean it," Sue said quietly, "but somehow I feel that that goes for you, too, Mother."

"You are being extremely rude and impertinent," Sue's father said.

"Is it rude," Sue said, her voice on the very edge of tears, "or impertinent to want your own mother there when you sing on a New York stage with the biggest name band in the country? Is it?" She came out on the porch then, not waiting for them to answer, and her eyes were bright with tears.

When we were up the street out of earshot, I said, "A

couple of chowderheads," meaning her parents. It was supposed to comfort her, but you can't please some people.

She took her hand away and said, "No one asked you, Johnny. This is a family affair, and you don't know anything about it." The Halls are a screwy family, fighting practically the whole time, but the back of their hand to an outsider who tries to get in the act. "Naturally Mother wants me on hand that day," Sue was saying. "The biggest day in her whole life."

"Some mother," I said, knowing I was on thin ice, but feeling that this should be said, that it should have been said months ago. "Oh, sure, she can quote you the latest statistics on juvenile delinquency in Upper Mongolia. She's all over the Day Nursery like a brooding hen, and the kids at the Rehabilitation Center call her Mom, but when it comes to a little garden variety maternal instinct—" That's as far as I got. Sue stopped dead in her tracks.

"That's all, brother," she said with terrible softness.

She lifted her hand, and I noticed how small and square her fingers were, the nails still cut short like a little girl's, and for no reason at all I wanted to hug her. She was so small and fierce, and so darned cute. She didn't actually slug me, but just before she turned on her heel to go home, she tarred and feathered me with a look.

That was two weeks before the Hall women's big day and, for the next two weeks, Sue wouldn't speak to me at school. Once I called her up and she said, "Have you anything to say?" Which in Sue's language means, "Are you ready to apologize?"

"Nothing special," I said. "I . . ." I was going to ask her for a date, but she hung up on me. I just plain couldn't apologize. It seemed to me that Mrs. Hall neglected Sue, and the Mother-of-the-Year deal made me mad.

153

The night before Sue was to go to New York, I strolled over to her house and, as I stood on the porch with my thumb an inch from the doorbell, I heard her mother and father talking.

"But, Jim," Mrs. Hall was saying, "seriously, do you think I'm a good mother?"

"I don't think I think of you as a mother very often," he said. "I think of you as a charming, intelligent, very pretty woman." He kissed her then, and it came as a shock to me. Old Man Hall, who was always yelling for blood, turning on the old schmalz! It was like Vesuvius erupting orangeade.

I guess I stepped on the squeaky loose board then—the one that Sue and I are always trying to bypass when we're a little bit late—because Mrs. Hall turned her head.

"That you, baby?" she called.

"No, Mrs. Hall," I said, feeling like Mata Hari in a T-shirt. "It's Johnny Hines." She got up and opened the door.

"Why, hello, Johnny," she said. "Sue went to Sharp's for some nail polish."

"She's discovered a shade called 'Gore,'" put in her old man. "You know—for the benefit of the guys in the second balcony."

I laughed, but not from the heart. I'd conjured up dreams of Billy Freeman smiling up at Sue. I'd faced the fact that there might even be a smile for the clarinetist. But the guys in the second balcony had escaped me until this minute. Nobody spoke for a long moment, and then Mrs. Hall put her hand on my sleeve.

"Johnny," she said, "maybe you'll be very honest with me. Do you think a mother has a right to an independent life? I mean, do you think it's all right for a mother to busy herself in community activities as I've been doing since

Cynthia and Joe got married, or do you think she should stay home and simply be a mother?"

I didn't really have to think before answering that. I'd thought about it too many times from so many angles. "I think," I said, "that there are times in people's lives for certain things. I think there's a time to be a mother, a long time maybe, depending on how many kids you have, and a time to do community things—" My voice sounded big and unpleasant there in the pretty chintz living room. For a minute I was sorry I'd opened my mouth; then Sue's mother spoke in a kind of faraway voice.

"All the chocolate layer cakes I used to make for the other children, and the shirts and blouses I'd iron any old time of the day or night. . . ."

"Oh, for heaven's sake, Petie, you sound like 'Portia Faces Life' or someone," Mr. Hall fairly shouted. "Anyone can bake a cake, but being able to set up a play center for those South Side youngsters—Why, of course you love Sue and she loves you. Gosh, she's so proud of you. . . ."

"That's not the same," Mrs. Hall said sadly. "Not the same at all. Is it, Johnny?" She didn't seem to expect an answer, for which I was grateful.

I knew she was going to cry, and that old man Hall was going to kiss her again, and I'm a hardboiled guy, but not *that* hardboiled. So I left quietly. Halfway to the village, I met Sue, and I knew I was ready to apologize.

"You know, your mother and father," I wanted to tell her, "why, they're not chowderheads at all. They're *people*." (In our crowd that's the highest praise there is.) I said, "Sue, I want to tell you something—" She looked at me as if I weren't there.

"I couldn't be less interested," she told me, and then she was gone, and I was watching her go: a skinny little girl in blue jeans and my old baseball sweater. A little brown-haired girl who walked like an Indian. And I wanted to spank her, but inside I was soft as a marshmallow.

"You knock 'em dead tomorrow, sugar," I said under my breath.

I knew that Sue was going to leave on the 11:42 next morning, and that a crowd from school was going to see her off. I'd made up my mind to drive into the city and surprise her by turning up in the front row, but for the first time in at least ten days, Nellie—that's my car—wouldn't start. She needs a new battery, but I've been trying to wheedle her along until I've paid for my class ring—which Sue is already wearing. I ran most of the way to the station but the 11:42 had gone, and there wasn't another train for an hour.

Practically no one goes to New York from Hamilton on Saturday, and I had the station all to myself. I weighed myself twice, because I was sure I was heavier than the first weight. Then I went into the phone booth and called Eddy Mason, just to kill time. I stopped talking when a train came roaring in on the northbound track and waited for it to pull out. But I never did finish my argument with Mason about who was the best batter in the National League, because after that things happened so fast that I'm just about now getting them all straightened out in my head.

A woman in a wide-brimmed hat was at the ticket window and, in the vacuum of silence that followed the train's pulling out, I could hear the ticket agent shouting, "Lady, there is absolutely no train to New York until 12:45." Then the waiting-room door burst open, and Sue Hall dashed in, making a beeline for the other phone booth, and I heard her saying, "Can you send a taxi to the station right this minute? Yes, this second."

Then she flew out and bumped smack into the lady with the wide-brimmed hat, and then . . . well, the lady turned out to be none other than Mrs. Hall, and the two of them did a doubletake.

"Sue—you missed your train!"

"No, I didn't, Mother, I got off at Prentiss and came back."

They were standing in the middle of the floor, their arms around each other, talking at the top of their lungs. "I was just on my way to the Paramount," Mrs. Hall said.

"I was tearing to the Woman's Club," Sue said then, and they both threw back their heads and laughed.

"Darling, I couldn't bear to think of you up on that stage without me there."

"I couldn't stand the thought of you at the luncheon and that terrible empty chair where I should have been."

I fanned myself with the timetable and prayed that they wouldn't see me.

"Oh, Susie, this was sweet of you," Mrs. Hall breathed. The 12:45 snorted in just then, and Mrs. Hall gave Sue a little push. "Come, baby," she said. "We'll be late, but Billy will understand."

"I telegraphed him that I couldn't come," Sue said. "You know, Mother, it's a silly thing, but I realized all of a sudden that I'd much rather be a big fish in a little pond. Golly, I don't have a New York kind of voice." (And here's a crazy thing—do you know that those were just about the prettiest words I'd ever heard in my life?) "What's more, Mother," she said, "I've a hunch Johnny isn't keen on singers." (On second thought, maybe *those* are the prettiest words.)

The taxi was outside beeping like mad. "Let's go," Sue said. "We can still make your shindig."

"I called the Mayor," Mrs. Hall told her. "Cynnie's going to receive the medal for me by proxy." They grinned at each other like two kids playing hooky, and then Mrs.

Hall said, "I think I'd like to be a big fish in a very small pond, if you'll help me."

"Oh, Mom," Sue cried in the nice cathedral tone that had heretofore been reserved for my home runs.

"Let's go to Louis'," Mrs. Hall said, "and have fried chicken and biscuits and fudge sundaes—"

"Oh, Mom," Sue said again, following her mother into the cab. "Mom, I do love you."

I emerged from my booth at that point, perspiring. The ticket agent jerked a head toward the door.

"Women," he intoned. "They're wonderful."

"Yeah," I said, looking forward to an era of chocolate cake and apple pie at the Hall household, and to picking up the paper without reading about Mothers of the Year and golden-voiced high school juniors; looking forward, too, to talking endlessly about baseball to a girl with brown hair who knows batting averages like other girls know fudge recipes, and who can hang on a guy's words like nobody's business.

"Wonderful," I said. "Especially my woman."

Written in the Stars

LOIS DUNCAN

Ever since I was very little, I knew that some day my prince would come. At first I used to envision him riding up on a snow white horse to scoop me up and carry me away to his castle. This changed, of course, as I grew older and my reading matter progressed from *Grimm's Fairy Tales* to *Romeo and Juliet*. I did away with the horse by the time I was eleven, but the rest of the belief remained, a quiet certainty deep inside of me. Somewhere in the world there was The One, the special One, looking for me just as I was looking for him, and someday he would come. It was written in the stars.

I never talked about it much, except once in a while to Mother. I dated just as the other girls did, strings of silly, uninteresting little boys, just to kill time until The One arrived. And then, when I was seventeen, two things happened. Mother gave me the locket, and I realized who The One was. Ted Bennington.

When I opened the little white package on my seventeenth birthday and saw the locket, I was flabbergasted. The locket was not a new purchase; I had seen it often before. In fact, every time I rummaged through Mother's jewelry box to borrow a pair of earrings or a bracelet or something, I saw it, not in the jumble of everyday jewelry but in the separate little tray where she kept all the things Daddy had given her. There was the whole story of a romance in that tray—Daddy's track medals from college and his fraternity pin, the pearls he gave Mother on their wedding day and the silver pin from their fifteenth anniversary and the silver bars he wore when he was in the Navy. And in the midst of all these things was the locket.

"But, Mother," I protested, holding it up in amazement, "you can't really mean for me to have this! It's yours. It belongs to you."

"Indeed I do," Mother said decidedly. "It represents a lot to me, honey. I've always said that my daughter would have it when she was seventeen." There was a faraway look in her eyes.

"But why seventeen?" I asked. "That's hardly a milestone. I mean, sweet sixteen is the age for first romance, and eighteen is the age of consent, but seventeen really isn't anything."

"It was to me," said Mother. "It was the age of heartbreak."

I stared at her in disbelief. "Your heart was never broken!"

It was impossible to imagine Daddy, with his warm gray eyes and gentle smile, ever breaking anyone's heart, least of all Mother's. Mother and Daddy had one of the best marriages I have ever known. They always seemed to have fun together, no matter where they were or what they were doing. And they loved each other. You could tell it just by being around them. It wasn't the grabbing, hanging-onto love of kids our age, but it went deeper; it was the sort of love that made Mother say two years ago when Daddy died, "Well, I've had more happiness in my eighteen years of marriage than most women have in fifty."

"Oh, it was broken, all right," Mother said lightly. "And yours will be too, dear. It's inevitable." She leaned over and kissed me.

I laughed, a little embarrassed, because we're not usually a very demonstrative family. Besides, I wasn't quite sure what Mother was talking about. But I did love the locket. It was tiny and heart-shaped on a thin gold chain, and it was delicate and old-fashioned and lovely. I felt about it the way Mother did about her engagement ring—"much too valuable just to wear around." I wrapped it in tissue paper and put it in the corner of my top bureau drawer.

The locket wasn't the only present I received on my seventeenth birthday. Besides that, Mother gave me an evening dress, ankle-length, dark rose taffeta, and Nancy, my best friend, gave me the rose slippers to wear with it. But the gift that topped everything, that caused my stomach to lurch and my heart to beat faster, was a simple blue scarf with a gold border. It came from Ted Bennington.

"I hope you like it," he said awkwardly. "I didn't know. I haven't had much experience picking things out for girls."

"I love it," I said warmly. "It's just beautiful."

I suppressed a desire to lean over and kiss him. It would have been so easy to do because I liked him so much. I liked the way his blond, curly hair fell forward over his forehead, and his honest blue eyes and nice, square chin. And I liked his being shy and sweet and serious and a little

161

awkward; it was so different from the smooth know-it-alls in our senior class. I thought, I *would* like to kiss you, Ted Bennington. But I didn't say it. And I didn't kiss him.

Instead I reached over and squeezed his hand and smiled at him and said, "It's beautiful," again. Which must have been the right thing to do, because he squeezed my hand and smiled back at me.

I had begun dating Ted a couple of months before that. It was funny how it started. Ted must have been in my class for years and years, and I never really noticed him. In fact, nobody noticed him. He was a quiet boy and he wasn't on any of the teams or in the student government or in any of the clubs; he worked after school and on weekends in Parks Drugstore. I think that might have been one of the things that made him shy, having to work when the other kids goofed around.

"It made me feel funny," he told me later, "having to serve Cokes and malts and things to the kids and then seeing them in school the next day. You can't actually be buddies with people who leave you ten cent tips."

"But none of the other kids felt like that," I told him. "They never gave it a moment's thought. They would have been glad to be friends any time if you'd acted like you wanted to."

"I know that now," Ted said. "But it took you to show me."

Which was true. It was cold-blooded in a way. I didn't have a date to the Homecoming Dance, and I was on the lookout for someone to take me. You don't have too much choice when you're a senior and most of the senior boys are going steady with juniors and sophomores. So I made a mental list of the boys who were left and crossed off the ones who were too short, and that left four. Ronny Brice weighs three hundred pounds and Steven Porter can't

stand me and Stanley Pierce spits when he talks. Which
left Ted.

"Do you know if Ted Bennington's asked anyone to
the Homecoming?" I asked Nancy.

Nancy gave me a surprised look. "Who?"

"Ted Bennington," I said. "The blond boy in our English class. The quiet one."

"Oh," Nancy said. "I didn't know that was his name.
No, I don't suppose he has. He doesn't date, does he? I've
never seen him at any of the dances."

"No," I said slowly, "I suppose he doesn't. But there's
always a first time."

The next morning I got to English class early and, as
Ted came in, I gave him a real once-over. I was surprised.
There was nothing wrong with his looks. He wasn't awfully
tall, but he had a nice build and good features and an
honest, clean-cut look about him. I even liked the back of
his neck.

Ted Bennington, I thought, you may not know it now,
but you are going to take me to the Homecoming Dance.

And I managed it. It is a little shameful to me now to
think about how schemingly I managed it—a smile here,
a sideways look there, "Hi, Ted," every time I passed him
in the hall, "What page did she say we were to do tonight,
Ted?" as we left class and happened to reach the door
together. A week or two of that and then the big step.
"Nancy's having a party this weekend, Ted, a girl-ask-
boy affair. Would you like to go?" It was really pretty
easy.

Ted was standing at his locker when I asked him. He had
the door open and was fishing out his gym shorts, and
when he turned he looked surprised, as though he were
sure he had not heard me correctly.

"Go? You mean with you?"

"Yes."

"Why—why, sure. Thanks. I'd like to." He looked terribly pleased and a little embarrassed, and I wondered suddenly if he had ever taken a girl anywhere in his entire life.

"What night is the party?" he asked now. "And what time? And where do you live?"

We stood there a few minutes, exchanging the routine information, and I began to wonder if maybe I was making a mistake asking Ted to the party, to that particular party anyway, because it would be The Crowd, the school leaders, the group I had run around with since babyhood. And Ted wasn't one of them.

But it was too late then, of course, to uninvite him, so I let it go, trying not to worry too much as the week ended, and on Saturday night at eight sharp Ted arrived at my house.

He made a good impression on Mother. I could see that right away. He had that quiet air of formal politeness that parents like. When we left Mother said, "Have fun, kids," and didn't ask, "What time will the party be over?" which is how I could always tell whether she really liked my dates.

Ted didn't have a car, so we walked to Nancy's, and it was a nice walk. Everything went off well at the party too. The Crowd seemed surprised to see Ted at first, but they accepted him more easily than I had thought possible. Ted relaxed after the first few minutes and really made an effort to fit in; he danced and took part in the games and talked to people.

Even Nancy was surprised.

"You know," she said when we were out in the kitchen together getting the Cokes out of the refrigerator, "that Ted Bennington—he's really a very nice guy. How come we've overlooked him before this?"

I said, "I don't know." I was wondering the same thing myself.

I wondered it even more as we walked home afterward, talking about the party and school and what we were going to do after we graduated: comfortable talk as if we'd known each other forever. I told Ted I was going to secretarial school, and he told me he was working toward a scholarship to Tulane where he wanted to study medicine. I learned that his mother was a widow, as mine was, and that he had three sisters, and that he played the guitar. The moonlight slanted down through the branches of the maples which lined the street, making splotches of light and shadow along the sidewalk, the air was crisp with autumn, and I was very conscious of my hand, small and empty, swinging along beside me. His hand was swinging, too, and after a while they sort of bumped into each other. We walked the rest of the way without saying much, just holding hands and walking through the patches of moonlight.

The next morning Nancy phoned to ask if Ted had invited me to the Homecoming.

"The Homecoming? Why, no," I said, "he didn't." And to my amazement, I realized that I had completely forgotten about the Homecoming—that now, somehow, it didn't matter very much.

When the time came, of course, we did go, but now that I think back on it, I don't think Ted ever did actually ask me. We just went, quite naturally, because by then we went everywhere together.

When did I realize that he was The One? I'm trying to remember. I guess there was no special time that the realization came. It just grew, a quiet knowledge deep inside me. It grew out of our walks together, long hikes through the autumn woods with the trees blowing wild and red and gold against the deep blue of the sky, and winter picnics

with The Crowd, sitting on blankets around a fire with
snow piled behind us and Ted's arm around my shoulders.
He brought his guitar sometimes to those, and we all
sang.

"Why didn't you tell us you played the guitar?" somebody asked him, and Ted grinned sheepishly and said, "I
didn't know anybody would be interested."

It grew, the realization, through the long, lovely spring
days and easy talk and laughter and a feeling of companion-
ship I had never known before with any boy or, for that
matter, with any girl, even Nancy. One Sunday evening
(we had been to church together that morning, and to the
beach all afternoon, and to an early movie after dinner)
Ted said, "We fit so well together, you and I," and I said,
"Yes," and he said, "It's as if it were meant to be that
way."

"You mean," I said, and the words came haltingly to
my tongue because I had never said them aloud to him
before and I was afraid they would sound silly, "You mean,
as though it were written in the stars?"

Ted was silent a moment and then he said, "Yes, I guess
that's what I mean."

It was the night of the Senior Prom that Ted saw the
locket. As I said before, I didn't wear it often, it was too
valuable, but somehow the night of the Senior Prom
seemed right. I wore my rose evening dress and my rose
slippers and no jewelry except the locket on its slender
gold chain.

Ted noticed it right away.

"Nice," he commented. "Makes you look sort of sweet
and old-fashioned. Is it a family heirloom?"

"More or less," I said. "Daddy gave it to Mother, and
Mother gave it to me." I touched it fondly.

Ted was interested. "Does it open?"

"I don't know," I said.

"Let's see." He reached over and took the locket in his hands, the gentle, capable hands I had grown to know so well, and fiddled with it a moment and it fell open on his palm, disclosing a tiny lock of hair.

"So," he said, smiling. "I didn't know your father had red hair."

"I guess he must have when he was young. He got gray very early." I smiled too. "Put it back, Ted. It belongs there."

He did so, closing the locket gently as though anything that had meaning for me had meaning for him also.

I'd tell you about the summer, but it is too hard to describe. I think you must know already what it's like to be in love. You get up in the morning and shower and dress and eat breakfast just as you always have before, but every motion, every ordinary thing, is flavored with excitement. "I'm going to see him today—in two hours—one hour—ten minutes—and now he is here!"—a warm glow inside you, a silent singing. That was the summer—and then, so terribly soon, it was autumn again.

Ted got his scholarship. His face, when he told me, was shining with excitement.

"How do you like the sound of it—*Doctor* Bennington!"

"Wonderful," I said. "Marvelous! But I'll miss you."

"I'll miss you too." He sobered. "I'll be home on vacations."

"Sure," I said. The summer loomed golden and glorious behind us; there would be other summers.

"I wish—" His voice trembled slightly. "I wish you were going to Tulane too."

"I'll be here," I said, "to come back to. I'll be a secretary in a year, you know. Maybe I can come up and get a job with some connection with the college."

"That would be great." Still he did not smile. "I'm afraid," he said suddenly.

"Afraid of what?"

"Of going. Of leaving you here. I'm afraid something will happen, you'll meet somebody else or something. What we've got, you and I—it's so right—so darned perfect! We can't lose it!"

"We won't," I said confidently. You don't lose something that is written in the stars.

So my prince rode away on his snow white horse, and that was the beginning of the end. We did not marry. If we had, I wouldn't bother telling this story. Ted went to college and I to secretarial school, and we wrote letters at first constantly and then not quite so often. Ted couldn't afford to come home at Thanksgiving, and when he did come at Christmas I had the measles (horrible thing to have when you're practically grown), and we did not really get to see each other until spring vacation. By then we had been so long apart that we spent the whole vacation getting reacquainted, and then it was time for Ted to go back again. He was as good and sweet and wonderful as ever, you understand; we just felt as though we didn't know each other quite so well.

"Don't forget me," he said a little desperately as he left.

And I said, "Of course not." But this time I did not sound so sure.

As it worked out, it was Ted who met somebody else; he who had been so worried, and I had been so sure! But in the end it was he who wrote the letter. The girl, he said, was a pre-med student just as he was. Her name—well, I've forgotten her name—but she was small, he said, and had hazel eyes and was smart and fun and easy to talk to. I would like her, he said, he knew. We were a lot alike in many ways. He said he was sorry.

It was raining the day the letter came. I read it in the living room and then gave it to Mother to read and went upstairs to my room.

I lay on the bed and listened to the sound of the rain and thought how strange it was, how unbelievable. I didn't hate Ted; you don't hate somebody as wonderful as Ted. I didn't even hate the girl. I was too numb to feel anything; I didn't even cry. I just lay there listening to the rain and thinking, he was The One—we were right—we fitted—we were perfect. Now he is gone and he was The One, and he will never come again.

I was still lying there when Mother came in. She did not knock, she just opened the door and came in and stood by the bed looking down at me. Before she said it, I knew what she was going to say.

"There will be other boys," she said. "You may not believe it now, but there will be."

"Yes," I replied, "I suppose so." There was no use arguing about something like that. "Ted was The One," I said. "There will be other boys, sure, but he was The One."

Mother was silent a moment. Then she said, "Do you still have the locket?"

"The locket?" I was surprised at the question. "Yes, of course, it's in my top drawer."

Mother went to the bureau and opened the drawer. She took out the locket and brought it over to the bed.

"Put it on," she said.

"Now?" I was more surprised. "But, why? Why now?"

"Because," Mother said quietly, "this is why I gave it to you." She put the locket in my hands and sat down on the edge of the bed, watching me as I raised it and put the chain around my neck and fumbled the tiny clasp into place. "You see," she said when I had finished, "that locket was given to *me* by The One on the evening of our engagement. We couldn't afford a ring right then. The locket had been in his family for a very long time."

"Oh." I reached up and touched the locket, feeling a new reverence for it. I thought of Daddy drawing it from his pocket, nervous, excited, watching Mother's face as he did so, hoping desperately that she would like it. Mother and Daddy—young and newly in love, two people I had never known and would never know.

"He was everything," Mother continued, "that I ever wanted in a husband. He was good and strong and honest, he was tender, he was fun to be with, and he loved me with all his heart. He was without doubt written for me in the stars." She paused and then added slowly, "He was killed in a train wreck three weeks after."

"He *what!*" I stared at her in bewilderment. "But you said—I thought—" I realized suddenly what she was telling me. "You mean it wasn't Daddy? You loved somebody before Daddy, somebody you thought was The One, and then—"

"I didn't just think it," Mother interrupted. "If I had married him I'm sure I would have been a happy woman and loved him all my life. As it worked out, three years later I married your father, and I have been a happy woman and loved *him* all my life. What I am trying to tell you, honey"—she leaned forward, trying to find the right words —"There is no One. There are men and there are women. There are many wonderful men who can give you love and happiness. Ted was probably one of them, but Ted just came too soon."

"But," I protested weakly, "that's so cold-blooded, so sort of—of—" I felt as though I were losing the prince on the snow white horse, the dream that was bright with the wonder of childhood.

"I'm saying," Mother said gently, "that there are many men worthy of loving. And the one of these who comes along *at the right time—he* is the one written for you in the stars."

She went out then and closed the door and left me alone, listening to the rain and fingering the locket. I stared at the door that Mother had just closed behind her.

And then I began thinking of the other door, the one she had just opened.

This Moment, Forever

ROBERT ZACKS

THE MOMENT she came up into the attic, Lila had an odd sense of being lost. She looked about the dim, musty room with the soft brilliance of north light coming through the slanted window, and wondered where to put the battered footstool she was carrying.

You'd think we would just throw it away, she thought, staring at the dusty clutter of boxes and discarded relics.

Things seemed to be waiting, brooding, in the attic. Slowly she recognized objects—an old bedspring, a broken fishing rod, old blankets they used for the car in winter. It was a history book of tangible things, and each seemed to have memories floating it toward Lila.

She thought, *Like a memory, that's what an attic is to a house, a memory of all that's taken place in it.*

Her fascination grew. Downstairs the house functioned

noisily toward dinner. In the sounds was a holiday gaiety, the joy of the Easter holidays. There was much to do that was wonderful, dressing in the pastel pinks and blues of new Easter outfits, the preparations for the Easter dinner which Lila's father firmly insisted must be roast turkey. She sat down before a huge cardboard carton and reaching inside idly pulled out a stiff, rectangular object covered with brown paper. She unwrapped it.

It was a picture of her parents. At first Lila didn't recognize them. The girl was as young as Lila was now. She laughed out of the snapshot, her eyes unclouded, full of the joy of living. Beside her was a young man who couldn't have been more than eighteen. They both held tennis rackets and . . .

An odd feeling of awareness came over her as she stared at the picture. It was as if she were not yet born and watched them from a secret place above. There they were, captured at that moment, forever, on a piece of paper . . . unaware that she, Lila, would some day be looking at them and thinking. . . .

The disturbing conversation she had with that new girl at school, Vivian, floated up from memory.

"No," Vivian had said in response to Lila's question. "You see, my mother died some years ago and my father has to travel on business all the time. So I won't be joining him for Easter. I'll stay here in town with my aunt."

A wave of embarrassment had swept over Lila.

"Oh, I'm sorry. About your mother, I mean," she said, her voice faltering.

Vivian looked surprised. "Oh, it happened many years ago. I'm used to it now." But her face showed hurt, sadness. It had bothered Lila terribly. As they walked through the bright air of middle spring with its wet warmth and promise of summer, an unease filled her. What was it like to have no mother?

She came home nervous and strangely afraid. She rushed into the kitchen where her mother was setting out supper dishes and flung her arms around her, kissing her fiercely.

"Goodness," cried her mother, laughing. "What's come over you? Oh, I know, your birthday."

Lila laughed, but her glance was hungry, searching. It was comforting to feel her mother's warmth, hear her laugh, see the wise smile.

As her eyes clung to her mother's face, the strange feeling faded and was gone. Here was Mother safe and the same as always, as she would forever be. The ground under Lila grew firmer.

"What's the matter, dear?" asked her mother quietly.

"I . . . nothing," she said. Her mother looked at her questioningly but said no more about it.

Up in the attic, now, Lila stared at the picture as if the young people in it would come alive and be her contemporaries, members of her gang at school, perhaps. It was strange and frightening that once they had been as she was now.

Pictures are terrible things, thought Lila, her heart hammering. *Every camera should be smashed. And there should be no birthdays with the awful feeling of getting older and older.*

From below her father called.

"Lila! Come down, will you!"

The table in the living room was set for three. Lila watched her mother carrying a bread dish and salt shakers in from the kitchen. As her mother stopped for a moment and cocked an eye at the table in artistic examination, Lila studied her face.

There was something different about the face, different from the picture in the attic. *What is it?* thought Lila unhappily. *What is it that makes the change?*

The face was tired. There were shadows under the eyes. . . .

"Hey," said Lila's father. "What kind of an inspection is this?"

Lila took a swift, agonized look at her father. His hairline was receding. There were wrinkles on his forehead and a faint thickening of his face, rounding it, burying its clean-cut, youthful lines. He, too, was changed.

She thought, *Some day they'll die and I'll be alone. It's something I can't stop.*

Her mother said quickly, "What's the matter, dear?"

Lila's eyes stung with the beginning of tears. As her parents moved toward her, anxiously ready with warm protection, she felt a wave of shame and dismay.

She couldn't possibly tell them her dreadful thought. To put it into words would be like . . . like considering it an awful, accomplished fact.

"Nothing, Mother," she said quietly. Her smile was quivering, but the tears receded. "I'm a little tired, that's all!"

"She's hungry, that's what," said her father cheerfully. "When do we eat?"

"Yes," said Lila quickly. "I'm awfully hungry."

"It won't be long," said her mother, going into the kitchen. Lila followed to help, and her mother gave her a warm smile as together they carried platters of food into the living room. From behind her forced briskness, her busy helping, Lila watched her parents, the life in them, the motions of their arms and the way they walked, the expressions on their faces, all so familiar, so seemingly eternal. It was impossible to believe that some day they would be gone, that just as her mother had once, long ago, had a mother of her own and gone through the incredible parting, so Lila would, too.

Involuntarily, the picture of the cemetery on Evergreen Street came to her mind. Each of those headstones represented a person who had breathed and walked and laughed and wept, mothers and fathers, all gone.

This time the tears came, spilling suddenly over the barrier of self-control. Lila kept her head bent, put down the platter she was carrying, and before anything could be noticed, turned and went swiftly toward the bathroom.

She was aware of their eyes on her back, puzzled and unsure. She locked herself in the bathroom and, leaning against the door, wept silently.

After a while she stopped. She carefully dried her eyes, but she couldn't do anything about the redness in them. She tried to think of an excuse.

She went out of the bathroom into the living room.

"Darling," cried her mother, "something *is* wrong. You've been acting so . . ."

"You've been crying," said her father soberly. "Haven't you, Lila?"

Lila said in a small voice, "I tried using mascara today. It got in my eyes."

The disbelief showed in their faces. Her father uttered a bark of laughter.

"Mascara," sighed her mother. "Well, you see what happens when you do such things. Now your eyes are all red."

"Still pretty, though," said her father.

They were making a quiet plea for her confidence, silently urging her to remember they were there to depend on if she wanted to discuss what was troubling her.

Lila turned her head away. It was not a thing she could bring up. Horror swept her at the thought.

177

Her father said with a too quick heartiness, "Let's eat. I'm starved."

It was a wonderful meal. The turkey was tender, delicious. As she ate, Lila stole glances at her parents, feeling the wonder of what she had always accepted as a commonplace thing.

And then it was over. The meal which had seemed, while it was under way, to be a thing that would and should last forever, was done. *As if it had never been*, thought Lila.

Her father held out the wishbone.

"Grab hold," he said, smiling.

"Make a wish first, dear," said her mother gravely.

Lila looked at them for a long moment. Then she thought, *I've made my wish*. She nodded, not trusting herself to speak.

"Pull," cried her mother, smiling.

They pulled. They twisted and tugged. Frantically, Lila clenched her hand on the slippery, tough bone. It wouldn't break. Her father increased his effort until the wishbone was pulled from Lila's hand, unbroken.

He looked at it ruefully.

"I guess we wished for the impossible," he said, laughing. "Let's give it another try."

Lila nodded slowly. She stared at her parents and took the wishbone end in her hand again. They pulled hard. It resisted and then split unexpectedly.

Lila had won her wish.

"You'd better not tell," said her mother solemnly, "or you don't get your wish."

Her father grinned at her, curiosity shining from his eyes.

Lila got up in a rush and went to her mother, kissing her fiercely. She smiled over her mother's shoulder at her father. He was watching Lila with that gentle, patient look of his.

It was almost as if he knew Lila's wish. She was going to hold back time as long as she could with her love for them, by relieving them of the worries that eat at vitality and vigor the way water silently eats away the strongest rock. She would always appreciate the wonder of being with them as she appreciated it right this very moment. She would do things to fill them with happiness, be more considerate. . . .

At this moment, a flash of beautiful understanding came to Lila.

Why, she thought in astonishment, *if we lived forever, if we weren't mortal, we wouldn't appreciate what we've got. It's the precious shortness of it that makes it so sweet. Is that why we need to love each other, to serve each other? Because time is so short?*

And then, as if in answer to a last troubling remnant of her old mood, there came the warm thought of children. Children, thought Lila, are immortality. You leave yourself behind.

"Why, Lila," said her father, wonderingly. "You know, you have a suddenly grown-up look. Whatever did you wish for?"

"Oh," said Lila quietly, "I made a practical wish."

Behold

JEAN FRITZ

BEFORE she was fully awake, Chris was aware of the peculiar hotel-smell of the room. She knew from the smell what the room would look like without opening her eyes or, for that matter, without trying to remember what it had actually looked like the night before when she and her mother and father had arrived in New York. She could see the flower arrangements hanging on the wall, the desk, its clean, blank blotter, the glass-topped bureau. She could see the emptiness inside the bureau drawers. Any other time it would have been pleasant, even exciting, to wake up in a strange, anonymous room, but not today. This was the last place Christine Wheeler wanted to be on the twenty-fourth of December.

She got out of bed, walked over to her suitcase and took out her diary. She would write in it now at the beginning of the day, she decided firmly, rather than at the end of the

181

day where Christmas Eve lay waiting like a desert to be crossed. Besides, the day would be just as truthfully recorded if she did it now. The day was planned; there was no hope of changing it. No hope at all.

Chris sat down at the prim little desk with its pigeonholes staring vacantly out at her. She opened her diary and set it adrift, face up on the bleak, green blotter. No hope. The words, if you said them slowly, had the long, lonely sound of a train whistle at night. Well, she had discovered something about hope in the last two days, a New Truth that was long and lonely sounding too. Chris unscrewed the cap of her pen.

"December 24. *New Truth:* Hope is a strange thing. Sometimes it is just as hard to fight against it as it is to fight for it.

"Today I must fight against it. I know, I *know* what the day will be. It will begin when Mother and Father wake up in the next room. We will go down to the coffee shop for breakfast and a waitress will serve us peroxide-blond eggs while we listen to a loud-speaker dreaming of a white Christmas. Father won't hear the loud-speaker; he will probably be buried in his papers, getting ready for Mrs. Boyle. The famous Mrs. Boyle. The horrible Mrs. Boyle from Baton Rouge, Louisiana, who had to come to New York now. Who couldn't possibly go to Europe any time except Christmas Eve. Who, of course, since she is his best client, must transact last-minute business with Mr. Douglas H. Wheeler, attorney from Boston, Massachusetts; father of Christine, fourteen years old, now fortunately too old to mind missing a Christmas at home."

Suddenly Chris put her head down on the blotter and, in spite of herself, went over again the conversation between her mother and father two nights ago when Mrs. Boyle had called. It was the telephone that had awakened her. At first she had tried to slough off the sound of her father's voice in the next room, but gradually words had detached themselves and forced their way through the walls into her consciousness. Unbelievable words.

". . . and all come to New York . . . and see you off at the airport . . . no . . . no . . . we'd be glad to . . . of course, for Christmas. . . ."

Then there had been the click of the receiver being replaced on the hook and Chris had waited for the denial, the reassuring explanation that her father would give her mother. Lying straight in bed, she had stared up at the cold, white ceiling and willed her father to laugh, to break the silence that was settling in the house like deep snow.

At last her father had spoken, but even now it was hard to connect that voice with her father. For a moment Chris had had the wild feeling that she had awakened as someone else in another house. Her father, who last summer in Canada had filled the trunk of the car with what he insisted was the perfect yule log, was talking now about Christmas in a voice colder than silence.

"There's nothing to look tragic about, Margaret," he had said. "One Christmas. After all, this is our bread and butter. Besides, Christmas gets more and more commercial . . . runs away with people. Maybe we need a little better perspective."

Her father spoke quickly as if he were chipping his words from a block of ice and not paying any attention to where they fell.

"Oh, don't—" Chris had whispered to the ceiling. "Don't."

But her father had persisted. "For heaven's sake, Margaret, Mrs. Boyle is more important than one Christmas celebration at home. Especially at our age. We'll spend Christmas Eve in New York and drive back on Christmas

Day sometime. Probably get there in the afternoon or evening. We can't do a thing about it, and what difference will it make anyway? One Christmas."

Chris had pulled the covers over her ears. One Christmas didn't make any difference, she had told herself. She could part with that. What mattered was *Christmas*—all Christmases. And in the next room her father had become a stranger, spoiling all Christmases in a cold, cold voice that she couldn't stop. Talking as if Christmas was something you outgrew. As if all these years he himself hadn't really cared. As if they had kept Christmas only to humor her.

"It isn't as if Chris were an infant," he had said. "We're a family of adults now and we don't have to trim the tree at exactly the same time and the same way every year."

Oh, but that had been the wonder—he had known that—repeating the same pattern because it was perfect, yet somehow making it more perfect by the repetition. Trimming the tree was part of it. Always they waited until the first star came out on Christmas Eve before they began. Always they started with the popcorn chains and ended at the top with the white and silver angel, so beautiful you could never quite remember from year to year how beautiful she was. Her wings and hair were blown back as if she had just alighted on the spire of the tree, breathless with the good news. When Chris was little, she had thought that at any minute the angel might really speak the words. "Behold," the angel would say, "I bring you good tidings of great joy. . . ."

Even as late as last year, Chris would not have been too surprised if the angel had spoken, but then she had always believed in miracles and what she secretly called Signs. She could never explain in words what she meant by a Sign. She just recognized one, as she recognized a New Truth, when she saw it. The closest she could come to describing a Sign, even to herself, was to say it was a happening perfectly timed like a rainbow and not only beautiful in itself but part of a bigger beauty. Even two days ago, Chris had to admit, it would not have been completely impossible for the Christmas tree angel to turn out to be a Sign. But now, of course, it was too late.

Chris slammed her diary shut and stood up abruptly. From now on, she was going to be adult. Very adult indeed.

The best way to be adult, Chris decided as she studied the menu at the breakfast table, was not to show your feelings. Better yet, not to have any feelings. Not even notice anything that would stir up leftover feelings. She held the menu high so she wouldn't have to notice her father's face, tired and unhappy-looking since yesterday morning. Her own face she arranged carefully before she lowered the menu and addressed the boutonniere of holly on the waitress' left shoulder.

"I'll have orange juice," she said, "scrambled eggs and toast."

Out of the corner of her eye, Chris could see her mother taking an aspirin tablet out of her pocketbook. Her father was drumming his fingers nervously on the table in time to a jukebox version of what else but *White Christmas.*

"And coffee," she added as a rather loud afterthought, and immediately regretted it. She could sense the surprised and amused glance being exchanged between her mother and father, but it was too late to retreat.

"Black," Chris added decisively, pleased at the short, hard sound of the word. If she said the word over and over to herself (black, black, black), perhaps she would not need to acknowledge the little invitations to gaiety being passed across the table by her mother and father.

"We've never seen New York at Christmas," her father was saying, pretending that Christmas still mattered. "You two will have a chance to do some sightseeing this morning while Mrs. Boyle and I do our business."

"We'll have all morning on Fifth Avenue," her mother said brightly. "We'll walk up the whole length of it. All those lovely store windows! Then we'll meet you and Mrs. Boyle for lunch at the Plaza. Is there anything special you'd like to do this morning, Chris?"

Chris looked over the top of her mother's little red hat, through the plate glass window at the sidewalk where an empty-eyed Santa Claus was waving the most hopeless-sounding bell she had ever heard.

Chris made her mouth into the shape of a small, neat smile. "I can't think of a thing," she said.

Outside a little girl had stopped and was staring into the face of the Santa Claus. He didn't see her. He went on waving the bell that sounded as if he had been lost at sea.

New York was full of the tolling of forlorn sidewalk bells, Chris discovered later. Walking up Fifth Avenue was like walking through circles of bell sounds. If you looked at the drooping, unkempt Santas in their cheap red costumes, it was not difficult to feel adult about Christmas. The difficulty came when you looked at the store windows.

Behind one, quiet as sleep, was a New England scene—a row of pointing pine trees, a white church, a house and a red barn, all resting under snow and a Christmas Eve sky. There was no doubt that it was a Christmas Eve sky. The family stood on their front steps and looked at it. The animals in the barn crowded at their open door and looked at it. Only a Christmas Eve sky could be so simple and so perfect. No spectacular planet systems were on display, no moon, no congested constellations. There was only a single star poised above a steeple like a flame above a candle.

Chris could feel her eyes smarting. That was *her* Christ-

mas behind the window, her house, her family on the front
steps, looking at the Christmas star. In a minute they
would go in and trim the tree and light the yule log, while
she stood outside on a noisy New York sidewalk and
watched them go.

"It's beautiful, isn't it?" Her mother's voice beside her
came as a shock. "Except for the barn, it's almost like us."

Like us as we *used* to be, Chris thought but she didn't
say it. She set her mouth into scissor-sharp lines so she
wouldn't say it, turned and looked into the unbearably
bright and brazen sunlight on Fifth Avenue—the angry
yellow taxicabs, the wheezing buses, the wooden-faced
Christmas crowds. Mumbling something about its being
late, she steered her mother away from the window, quickly
away, into the crowd moving step by step farther away.
Once she looked back and over her shoulder caught a last
glimpse of the white steeple pointing to the star. Then it
was gone and Chris was part of the army of mechanical
legs marching up Fifth Avenue. Past Forty-sixth Street,
Forty-seventh, Forty-eighth. One, two, three, four. Her
feet and her mother's kept perfect time.

Her mother chattered about inconsequential things as
they walked, her words bobbing so innocently between
them that Chris let them just come and go without really
listening—one, two, three, four—and hardly answering. She
almost let the important sentence slide away with all the
unimportant ones.

"You know, Chris," her mother said. "You're just like
your father."

Even then Chris didn't miss a step. "What do you mean
—like Father?"

"Oh, the way you turn cold when you're hurt or disappointed. Your father does the same thing. Not the way
he did when I first knew him. But sometimes he still does

without meaning to or wanting to. Like you're doing. You should have heard him the other night when Mrs. Boyle called!"

They were in front of St. Patrick's Cathedral. Chris looked at the steps banked with pigeons squatting and staring blankly out at the street as if nothing of interest could happen there. Being New York pigeons, they would never fly.

"What did he say?" Chris asked.

Her mother laughed. "Oh, the silliest things! What difference did it make about Christmas at our age and we are a family of adults now. Imagine! Why, he doesn't even trust anyone else to cut down our Christmas tree."

They were almost past the cathedral steps and not a single pigeon had moved. They went on sitting stupidly as if they didn't know they had wings.

"Maybe he's grown tired of Christmas," Chris said.

"Tired of it? Your father? Don't be silly. No, it was a first reaction. A way to hide his disappointment for a moment even from himself. Pretending he didn't have feelings."

Mrs. Wheeler looked up at the long line of the cathedral leaning into the sky. "You know, Chris, growing up doesn't stop when you're grown up. When I was your age, I used to think it did."

They walked to the corner and waited for the light to change. Mrs. Wheeler laughed fondly. "Why, Christmas means so much to your father," she said, "that it never even occurred to him that we could spend Christmas separately. I don't believe it entered his head that he could come to New York alone, the way he always does when he sees Mrs. Boyle. No, as far as he was concerned, it was bad enough to change Christmas; it would have been unthinkable not to have had it together."

Suddenly Chris wished she could run back to the cathedral steps and send those forlorn city pigeons up in the air. She would run through their lines, clapping her hands for them to go higher and higher until they reached the very top of the cathedral.

Instead the light changed and Chris walked across the street with her mother, feeling strangely out of breath as if she really had run back to the cathedral steps, as if she were still running to catch up to—what? She didn't know. To something that didn't have words yet. To feelings and thoughts tumbling about which she didn't have time to sort out on Fifth Avenue with the Rockefeller Plaza Christmas tree rising at one moment so unbelievably tall beside her, and at the next moment the enormous golden Atlas, straining to hold up a world that didn't look so heavy, after all.

If she were at home now, it would be different. She would close herself in her own room with the pink-flowered wallpaper she knew by heart on all sides of her. She would spread out her mother's conversation, word for word, and the long walk up Fifth Avenue, block by block, beside all the past facts and feelings and understandings in her possession and after a while she would come up with a New Truth. That was the way you came upon Truths—unexpectedly in the midst of experience, hidden in conversations. You unraveled and you pieced together and when you found one—well, there it was, unmistakable as rock, waiting to be entered in your diary in the hope that some day, possibly, there might be enough little Truths that could be added up like a column of firm figures. And there at last would be the Whole Truth.

But now she was in New York and approaching that moment on Fifth Avenue that she always liked best—when suddenly, impulsively even, the street drops one whole tall side of buildings to make way for the park. Here under the stony eye of General Sherman was the usual cluster of hansom cabs with their blanketed horses and top-hatted drivers ready to take you back to 1890. And here also, Chris reminded herself, was the Plaza Hotel, waiting to bow her down its stealthily carpeted halls to lunch, according to plan.

Chris did not question those plans. She expected to go through the hotel door, she expected to hoist up little flags of politeness all afternoon for Mrs. Boyle, but then a taxi door slammed shut behind her and all the unchangeable plans were changed. Mr. Wheeler stepped out of the taxi and, instead of meeting inside with Mrs. Boyle, the three of them found themselves together on the sidewalk in that sudden and unexpected way that makes a person immediately want to find other sudden and unexpected things to do. Mr. Wheeler looked at his watch. They didn't really have to go in yet, he said, if they didn't want to. He pushed his hat slightly to the back of his head in a quick way that made him look young and casual, hardly like a father at all.

"I've just been to the bank for Mrs. Boyle and I'm back sooner than I thought I'd be. She's not expecting us quite yet." A smile started in his eyes and spilled over his face. "Let's run away for half an hour. I don't know where, but it doesn't matter." He tipped his hat a fraction of an inch farther to the back of his head. "It's the day before Christmas and almost anything can happen. Almost anywhere. Let's look for something."

Chris felt as if the yule log had just been placed in the fireplace and the first match held to it. "Let's go to Central Park," she said.

It was quiet in the park. They left the sidewalk in favor of a bridle path that wound such a leisurely, country course, it was hard to believe where they were. For a split second Chris could even see the people in the world—weeping and laughing, growing up, stumbling and getting up again —all the children and the mothers and fathers, the old men and the old women, and she felt sorry and loved them, each one, in a way she didn't understand and could hardly bear.

Then it was over and the world, instead of being so painfully wide, was one fir tree in front of her. A beautifully shaped tree, the kind that her father had already cut and that was waiting for them at home. Under the tree were two little boys dressed rather formally in gray leggings, matching coats and jackets. Between them, set firmly on the ground, was a large brown paper bag from which the boys were lifting small plastic crèche figures. Mary and Joseph and the Babe were already in place beneath the tree. The older boy took out a donkey with three legs and tried to balance him beside the manger. The donkey kept toppling over and at last the boy pushed the three legs slightly into the ground. Planted this way, the donkey stood staunch beside Mary and the boy smiled.

"Put the shepherds way over there," the boy pointed to his brother. "That will be their field. And over on this side will be the Wise Men."

Chris and her mother and father stood as one person, still and at a little distance, so as not to startle the children. The shepherds were in their field now, leaning on their crooks, looking up at the blue New York sky. On the opposite side two Wise Men (the third was apparently lost) were astride their camels on the road to Bethlehem, a busy road which they shared with an unrehearsed pilgrimage of gray New York pigeons.

The older boy took his hands away from the Wise Men.

191

"No," he said gravely. "The shepherds should go first. They've seen the star. So you move your shepherds up, John."

Chris held her breath. She felt as if she were standing with her mother and father on their doorstep at home. She slipped her arms through theirs and watched the shepherds take their place, one by one, in front of the crèche. The first Wise Man moved up, the one with the myrrh, and after him the second Wise Man with his bag of gold.

Then suddenly among the gray park pigeons picking their way toward the stable, there was a whir of wings. A small, white pigeon flew straight up into the air and lighted on top of the tree, fluttered once or twice to make sure of his balance, and then held still, his wings folded back— white with silver streakings.

There were no words for what was happening. It was like standing in the middle of a Truth so big there would never be any words for it.

Chris looked at the lovely white bird, swaying so gently on the tip of the tree.

"Behold," she whispered softly to herself. "Behold. . . ."

Another Spring

MICHAEL SHAARA

WHEN IT was all over they walked off alone, hand in hand, and sat down under a fine dogwood overlooking the valley. The dogwood was just coming into flower; from where they sat they could see the whole valley spread soft and cool beneath them, turning green even as they watched. The girl stared down into the valley without seeing it. She was very young and blonde, and the mourning in which she was dressed did not become her. She was too young for black, too young almost for the husband beside her, who was himself not much older.

They sat silently together, still holding hands. There was nothing to say. Her father was buried and the tears had come and gone. There was only this long last pause on this warm afternoon, and then they would go down again to their own home and this part of their lives would be over.

The husband watched the girl quietly. He knew that to heal the wound she had to talk, but he was silent. He had loved the old man himself and he could imagine what it must be like for the girl. The old man was all the kin the girl had ever had. Her mother had borne her late and died of it, and the girl had grown up alone with her father on this little farm. She took care of him in that fine, fussy way a daughter has, and though he shaped her gently but with great care to want a family of her own, she insisted she would never leave him.

When she was nineteen and she met this young man, the torture began. The old man insisted from the first that she leave. He said he could take care of himself very well and that it was a shameful thing for her to waste her life as servant to such an old man. But she would not go. She argued, she fought, the young man appealed, a year passed.

And then she came down one day and met the young man in town and married him. Exactly what had changed her mind the young man never knew. Or cared. He was enough in love to believe love had done it, but he also felt grateful to the old man. They went out to see him often in the fall and winter of that year, and then in the spring he died.

So the young man thought now that his wife was blaming herself for leaving. He wanted to talk about that but he did not. He waited.

After a while the girl leaned back against the slim bole of the tree. She stared up at the white flowers and he saw her face begin to crumple, as if she would cry. But she did not, and in a moment he saw that her face was soft and still again.

"What are you thinking?" he asked.

"About the dogwood." She went on gazing up at the tree. "This was my tree. Did I ever tell you that?"

He shook his head.

"It was always my tree," she said softly. "When I was about twelve my father took me to a nursery, and while we were there the man gave me this tree, a little seedling in a can. He told me to take it home and give it shade and I was—oh, I was delighted. It was my own little tree. My father loved trees. That one there—you see that huge oak? —that was his tree, and this was mine."

The young man looked where she pointed and saw a great old oak standing alone on a small knoll. He looked back to the girl and she was smiling.

"I remember I planted it as soon as I got home. I put it right up close under the oak, almost against the trunk. My father warned me that it wouldn't grow well there, but I wanted it close to his tree. And besides, the man had said to give it shade. It did very well, though it's a wonder I didn't kill it; I used to put fertilizer on it about once a day. But my father would come out afterward and take care of it, and he was very good with growing things. Everyone said he made this little farm produce more than any man could have."

"He grew you," the young man said. He squeezed her hand.

"But I never should have planted it there. It did well for a while—I remember the first time it bloomed. I used to do dishes and look out the big kitchen window and see both trees, the great big one shading the little one and the little one all in bloom, all white, and it made me feel very good. My father liked it too, but most of all he loved that oak. It was the biggest tree for miles around, and every now and then the lightning hit it. That always made

195

my father mad. Lightning always strikes the highest point and so it hits the big trees first, and my father said that was a terrible shame—the price a tree pays for outgrowing its neighbors. . . ."

The girl turned her eyes down into the valley. The young man sat still. After a moment she looked at him.

"You won't think I'm silly?"

He smiled.

"I never told you this before. About that last week before we were married I—you mustn't think I'm silly."

"I love you."

"Yes, but it was never anything—to talk about. It was very bad, that last week. I wonder if you ever really knew. I couldn't leave him, I couldn't, and yet I loved you so much and he wanted me to go. He kept explaining all the time that I hurt him by staying, made him feel terrible that he was keeping me from a life of my own. And yet even in that he was gentle; he never forced me. And I couldn't leave, not until that one last day—because of the tree. You see?"

The young man waited.

"Well, that day two men came up to our house and my father went out to meet them and I saw them gather around the oak. I went to find out what they were doing, and my father said they were going to move the dogwood. Well, I was on edge anyway, but I loved that tree and I was badly shaken. I hated to have them move it but my father said, 'Look at it; it's in too close to the oak. The roots are all grown together and they're robbing each other. The dogwood needs more sun now, and the old oak has had too much lightning and needs nourishment from the ground. If they stay here together, it will ruin them both.'

"And he was right; of course he was right. The dogwood was already twisted and out of shape, straining to get away from the oak, and the old tree was tired. Even so, I ran away to my room crying because I saw that too many things were changing; nothing was the same.

"And then later that afternoon I looked out and saw the dogwood on this hill where it is now, all alone and looking strange, and suddenly it wasn't my dogwood any more. It wasn't—the same. And the oak was different too, scarred in front by the hole they'd dug to lift the dogwood. And then I saw what my father meant—that we couldn't grow that way, neither we nor trees nor anything. And looking at the dogwood I knew he was right and I had to go. And that day I came down to you."

She stopped and stared at him, her eyes filling with tears.

"He was such a fine man," she said. The young man reached out and held her silently, soothingly, stroking her hair; but looking down past her shoulder, he could see the great oak, and he felt a massive chill. He was a man who knew something of trees, and he saw that though the other trees had begun to bud, the oak had not. And he thought: The old man knew that. He must have known it. When he transplanted the dogwood, he had to take a great ball of earth with it, all the young roots, and many roots of the oak had to be cut and torn away. But it was an old tree scarred by lightning and it could not stand the loss. And so it died, and the old man knew it would die—blessed old man. But he went ahead and dug up the tree and sent his daughter away, sacrificing the oak for the dogwood and knowing it, sacrificing himself for his daughter and knowing that, too, for neither tree nor man could survive the loss.

The young man thought for a long while. I must never tell her that, he thought. He kissed the blonde head. No, the old man would never have wanted her to know.

Too Young to Marry

JOHN D. MacDONALD

IT WAS July again, one whole year since the strange offer had been made and accepted.

Walter Harrison sat heavily and alone on the screened porch and wondered how this evening would end. He could hear his wife, Mary, restlessly cleaning the spotless living room for the tenth time.

She had been almost relentlessly gay this evening, and he knew how much courage that had taken. He could hear the younger members of the family playing out behind the house in the warm dusk. They had been ordered to stay out of the way.

James and Elizabeth Rawlings would arrive within a half hour. The two couples would be fidgety and awkward with each other, as before.

A little while later the others who were in love would

come and tell the two sets of parents of their decision. And because of the odd agreement the parents had made with them, it would be too late for the exercise of parental authority—too late to save quiet, steady, eighteen-year-old Jud Harrison from the mistake he would regret the rest of his life.

Last July, a year ago, Jud had come to him bringing Nancy Rawlings along, to tell him that they wanted to be married. They were both seventeen. They had just finished their junior year in high school. Jud had been flushed, level-eyed, frighteningly serious.

Nancy, though full of nervous smiles and unaccountable gigglings, had that same ominous quality of resolve. Though greatly shocked, Walter Harrison was glad that he had sense enough to tell them he was glad they had come to him about it instead of running off.

Walter passed along his feeling of shock and alarm to Mary. Then the two seventeen-year-olds went and made the same call on Jim and Betty Rawlings. And Jim, in white anger, made some comments to Jud that Jud did not care to repeat to his father. Walter sensed the spirit of rebellion in the two, and he phoned Jim Rawlings and tried to set up a conference among the four parents.

Walter knew Rawlings casually, knew that he owned and operated an appliance store on Main Street, knew that the two families were about in the same income bracket. Nancy was their eldest child, as Jud was the first-born of the Harrisons.

He knew that Jim, a lean, nervous-acting man, had a reputation for a quick temper. At first Jim didn't want even to talk about it. He said it was too darn ridiculous to talk about, and anyway Betty was far too upset to be a party to any absurd conference about it.

Walter kept his temper and cajoled Rawlings into meeting him for lunch. Jim Rawlings at lunch was white-lipped. "They're kids. They'll get over it. I'm ordering Nancy not to see that boy of yours, and I expect you to do the same."

"Dandy!" Walter said heavily. "Just fine. Shall we chain them to posts in our back yards? Both of them have spirit, thank God. And if we put the lid on, we'll get a wire or a phone call from Georgia after they run over there and get married."

"Nonsense!"

"Can't you remember how it was at seventeen, Jim? First love? It really hits you. I'm confident we're on the wrong track. They'll run off."

"Can't you control that boy of yours?"

Walter stiffened and then, with an effort, curbed his anger. "Are you sure Nancy will obey you?"

"She's reasonable," Jim admitted. "But she's got a stubborn streak."

Walter leaned forward and said, "Our only chance is to buy time. Enough time so there'll be a good chance of their breaking up before they do something silly."

Rawlings agreed at last and the plan was devised and, after much discussion, the two mothers agreed to it. The four parents met with Jud and Nancy, and Walter Harrison acted as spokesman while the kids sat, hand in hand, wary and subdued.

"We think you're both too young. We think you ought to wait. At least a year. But we know we can't pin you down that way without creating resentment. Jim and I have decided on a proposal: We know you're both practical. You've both had spare-time jobs and summer jobs. Jim and I will each set aside one hundred dollars a month in a special account for you two. With taxes and expenses, it won't be easy for us, but we talked over the figure and we can do it.

"Each month you wait, you'll be saving two hundred dollars for your future. If you wait the full year, you'll have twenty-four hundred dollars to begin married life on. We would both have preferred to spend that money on your education, but that will be your choice. We've all agreed to it and we want you to think it's fair."

Jud frowned and said, hesitantly, "Like if we wait until . . . say Christmas, there would be about a thousand dollars? We could have that then?"

"Correct," Rawlings said curtly.

Nancy and Jud glanced at each other and Nancy said in her thin voice, "We think we ought to talk it over."

"Of course, dear," her mother agreed.

The kids agreed to accept and agreed to wait an indeterminate period, wait until they felt the time had come and then give fair warning.

That night in the bedroom darkness, Mary whispered to Walter, "They're so . . . young. Will it work, darling?"

"I think so. A year is a very long time. Those things end quickly. They'll break up. We're just buying time."

"She isn't right for Jud. She's shallow and she's selfish. If she were right for him, she'd be thinking of his future."

"Don't worry, honey," he said. "Just try not to worry."

But there had been no quarrel. Christmas had been a crucial time, but the two did not make their decision then. They were close, inseparable, through their senior year. They both graduated with good grades, walked together at graduation, went to the senior dance together; both found summer jobs—and both were now eighteen.

At least, Walter thought, we bought that much for them, paid for that much time. Now they said they had made a decision and they wanted a conference as before, Jud and Nancy and the four parents.

Walter knew they would now wish to be married. He knew that as a matter of honor, of having given his word, he would have to accept it. And they were too young, too vulnerable, too unprepared for life. Life was full of rude shocks, and they did not yet have the proper weapons of defense.

The gamble had not worked, and Walter was afraid that Rawlings would now try to back out of the agreement. Walter was not particularly heartened by his belief that it was the only thing they could have done.

He stood up when the car stopped in front and Jim and Betty Rawlings came up the walk in the July dusk.

Mary came out onto the porch. The four of them sat there tensely.

"It didn't work out," Rawlings said accusingly.

"Not the way we hoped," Walter said.

"Before they spring it on us," Jim said, "I want to say one thing. We made the gamble. I think we ought to stick with it. I'll help them as much as I can. You plan to stick to the agreement, Walt?"

Walter Harrison smiled and suddenly liked Jim Rawlings better. The man had a code of decency. And was shrewd enough to know that to back out would mean the end of all respect. Jim might make a very acceptable father-in-law for Jud.

"I'll stick to the agreement," Walter said.

"I thought it would be so long before my daughter would be a bride," Betty Rawlings said. "I hoped she'd marry—" She stopped abruptly, and they knew what she was about to say and shared her embarrassment. Hoped she'd marry a man who could support her nicely.

"Nancy is a sweet girl," Mary Harrison said firmly, and Walter was proud of her for saying it. The two couples felt

closer, but there was no flavor of gaiety. Nancy and Jud
were too young to marry. It was something to face, to feel
sorry about. It was a death of many hopes.

The two arrived ten minutes later and came up the
walk to the house. They all went into the living room and,
as before, Jud and Nancy sat together on the couch. They
looked so serious and so young. Their nervous smiles were
a little too mechanical, but Walter saw that Nancy wasn't
so jittery as before. There was a new quality of repose about
her, a hint of maturity.

"So now we get the news," Jim Rawlings said too heart-
ily.

"Yes, sir," Jud said. "We think it's swell, the way you've
been, the money and all. Maybe you thought we wouldn't
stay together for all this time. Maybe you thought it was
just . . . kid stuff. But it's been a year and it's going to
be a lot of years."

Nancy nodded firmly.

"And so now you want to be married?" Mary Harrison
said gently.

"Well . . . we have a sort of counter offer," Nancy
said. "We . . . you'd better tell them, Jud. I mean, ask
them."

Jud looked down at his hands and then looked at them
all, turned his eyes at last to his father, steady, gray eyes.
"We're as certain as we ever were, but maybe we aren't in
so big a rush. I mean we were only seventeen last year.
We've done a lot of talking—about the future and what
we'll do and what kind of a life we want to have."

"We think we should wait a little while longer," Nancy
said. "I'm sorry, Jud. I interrupted."

"You don't have to keep putting the money in. We're
not asking for that," Jud said. "We can both get into State.
I've been writing to Student Aid, and we've got two part-